The Blood of the Wine

a novel

DARYLL SIMCOX

The Blood of the Wine
Daryll Simcox
Published April 2026
Little Creek Books
Imprint of Jan-Carol Publishing, Inc.

Graphic Design: Tara Sizemore

ISBN: 978-1-970471-28-1 (Paperback)
ISBN: 978-1-970471-29-8 (Hardcover)
Library of Congress Control Number: 2026936008

You may contact the publisher:
Jan-Carol Publishing, Inc.
PO Box 701
Johnson City, TN 37605
publisher@jancarolpublishing.com
www.jancarolpublishing.com

Once again, I would like to thank each and every one of you for taking the time to read my third book. The first two books–about the Hairy Man of Port Chatham, Alaska–were a real pleasure to write, but something about creating a story that involves the very place that I call home really intrigued me. I hope everyone enjoys reading THE BLOOD OF THE WINE *as much as I did creating it. Never take for granted what could be watching just beyond the vision of one's eyes. Just maybe, the mythical creature of your nightmares is lurking in the shadows of the darkness... waiting for the moment to attack.*

ALSO BY DARYLL SIMCOX:

The Breath of Darkness

(Book 1)

Under Watchful Eyes

(Book 2)

PROLOGUE

A long time ago, a creature walked through the shadows of the forest during the darkness of the night. Only the light of the moon provided an insight as to what was moving between the trees. The sounds of the things that could not be seen only added to the fear of anyone who dared to walk the darkened paths of the forest. How this evil could once again come to life in a land so far away was beyond the imagination of so many. But now, this creature not only lives in our minds as we dream late at night; it walks the very land we commonly call home. For the individuals that face the daunting task of determining the existence of such a creature, the journey is beyond their wildest dreams, and the paths they must travel to find it will be filled with a darkness of their own.

CHAPTER 1

Just a few minutes past 11 in the morning, the call came on the radio. There was an injured hiker on the mountain next to the parking lot at Clingmans Dome. As Sonny Rutherford exited the Sugarlands Visitor Center, he caught sight of Billy Rogers opening his familiar white-and-green-striped park ranger pickup truck. Immediately, he raised his hand and gave a shoutout to Billy, who turned and responded by asking Sonny to jump in.

As Sonny shut the door and fastened his seatbelt, he said, "Thought I might just ride with you if that's okay... I've already been up and down this mountain three times today."

Billy looked at Sonny and smiled. "Sounds good to me, Chief. I've only made two trips so far."

Billy always called Sonny "Chief" because he was half Cherokee Indian and had remained close to his heritage of the Cherokee Indians on the other side of the mountain. The Cherokee Indian reservation remained the same as it had almost from the beginning when it became a tourist destination, except for the casino that was constructed for all the individuals dreaming of hitting it big one day.

Sonny's mother was full-blooded Cherokee, and his father was one of the construction workers that helped build the small, quaint motels that still inhabited the area on the sides of the streets along with the small stores that sold the handmade merchandise. Sonny's mother and father had both passed away—two people he so dearly missed.

Billy Rogers was much younger than Sonny, a fact that he liked to rub in Sonny's face whenever he got the opportunity. At 25 years of age, Billy was finally able to land the ranger job at the Great Smoky Mountains National Park. This was a place his family visited every year for their family vacation, a place he had fallen in love with as a kid. His mother still came to visit at least once a year and sometimes twice. Billy's father had passed away suddenly when he was 19. For the last five years, Billy had tried to convince his mother to come to the area. He hoped that someday his efforts would finally pay off and she would come to live either with him or close by. In a way, Billy had kind of adopted Sonny as a father figure. Sonny and his wife didn't mind that at all, since they had never had any children of their own.

The ride from the visitor center to the top of the mountain at Newfound Gap was always peaceful for Sonny, even more enjoyable when one was peering out the window instead of constantly watching the traffic ahead. Once Billy reached the Gap, he made the right turn for the drive to Clingmans Dome. With each turn of the winding road, both men kept a watchful eye for anything that indicated an injured hiker ahead.

Finally, as the parking lot came into view, the men spotted the small crowd gathered where the trail began at the edge of the pavement. Billy slowly pulled the truck next to the group of people and placed the vehicle into park; he and Sonny exited the ranger truck to assess the situation.

The lady was sitting on a large rock, and her husband had acquired a small bag of ice. He was holding the bag against the outside portion of her ankle. The melting ice was running down her foot and dripping onto the ground where she sat. A small puddle had already formed there.

Just as the two men knelt beside her, the lady looked at Sonny and smiled. "Am I your first clumsy tourist of the day?" she asked.

Everyone around them laughed, then Billy asked, "How bad is it, ma'am? Can I take a look?"

As the man removed the bag and Billy began to study the injury, the woman placed her hand on Billy's shoulder and winked at the crowd. "Been a long time since a man your age played with that ankle," she said.

Billy turned bright red and shook his head. Sonny and the woman's husband laughed as the crowd began to disperse. The husband stretched his hand out to Sonny. He said, "We think it's just a sprain... She rolled her foot off the edge of a rock, but luckily, I caught her before she fell to the ground. I don't know who made the call, but we do appreciate you guys coming all the way up here."

Sonny shook the man's hand. "Not a problem, sir, we want to make sure that she's okay."

The woman still had her hand on Billy's shoulder. "I believe I'll be okay if you guys can just help me to the truck. In fact... I think it would be a lot better if you carried me, young man."

Once again, Billy just shook his head, and the other two men chuckled. Billy then looked at Sonny and said, "I believe she's just twisted her ankle." Then he turned to the woman. "If I carry you to your vehicle, will you promise to go to a medical facility and have them check the ankle to be sure?"

The woman squeezed Billy's shoulder. "Absolutely, young man. Will you be available to carry me from the motel to a restaurant this evening?"

Sonny gently poked the husband's arm. "Oh yes, ma'am. I will personally see to it."

The woman smiled as she placed her arm around Billy's neck. Next, he slid his right arm under her knees and supported her back with his left arm. Gently, he raised the lady from the rock and followed the husband to the red pickup truck. The husband unlocked the door and Sonny assisted with getting the woman buckled into her seat. Billy pointed his finger at the woman and reminded her that she promised to have the ankle checked out.

She promised that she would, and once again they thanked the park rangers for their help.

The two rangers returned to the park ranger vehicle, and once they were buckled in, Billy started the engine. Sonny had a big grin on his face as he stared out the window.

Billy turned to Sonny and tilted his head. “Okay, just what are you smiling about, Chief?”

Sonny looked over and raised his eyebrows slightly. “I think that woman was a little sweet on you, Billy.”

Billy put the truck into gear. “Yeah, I noticed that you and her husband got a big kick out of her embarrassing me.”

Sonny laughed, “You turned blood red, Billy. It’s always much more fun when it happens to someone else.”

Billy replied, “Glad you had a little fun at my expense. Maybe I should have left you down at the visitor center.”

As the men started back down the road to Newfound Gap, they encountered several vehicles making their way to the parking lot for Clingmans Dome. Even though it was really difficult to see very far from the structure during the summer months, for many visitors of the park, it was definitely on their bucket list of things to do. The haze that filled the air during this time was what gave the park its name; it also helped with the numerous thunderstorms that, at times, popped up without any warning. For the tourists who came here, it was a magical place that would draw most of them here again and again.

As soon as Billy and Sonny arrived at the stop sign bordering route 441, they were met with a steady stream of vehicles coming from both directions. Both men were focusing left and then right, repeatedly looking for an opening. It was quickly closing in on the end of May, and the tourist season was now in full swing. Of course, nowadays, it didn’t really seem that there was such a thing as an off season.

Suddenly, the opportunity presented itself, and Billy pushed the accelerator with his boot. In the blink of an eye, the men were headed back off the mountain toward the visitor center. Billy glanced over at Sonny and said, "Good thing I was driving, Chief... Somebody your age probably wouldn't have had the reflexes to make that move."

Sonny responded, "Probably not, Billy... You just about gave me a heart attack there."

Billy laughed, "Looks like it's gonna be another busy summer, Chief."

Sonny was observing all the vehicles making their way to the top of the mountain. He said, "I don't know how, but it seems like more people show up each and every year."

The men passed the parking lot for the hike to the famous Chimney Tops. There wasn't an empty spot. After passing the Chimney's picnic area, the road began to straighten out somewhat as the men made their way off the mountain. Just above the Sugarlands Visitor Center where the Husky Gap Trail intercepts the road, Sonny spotted a young man frantically waving both arms. He instructed Billy to pull over.

As Billy placed the truck in park and set the emergency brake, he stated, "This doesn't look good, Chief."

The two men had barely closed the doors to the vehicle when the man came running up to them. He placed both hands on his knees and was gasping for each breath he took. Between his efforts of sucking in the fresh mountain air, the young man tried to talk to Billy and Sonny.

"We... found somebody... up in the woods," he gasped.

Sonny took ahold of the man's arm, and Billy knelt in front of him. "Are they hurt? Can you take us to them?"

The young man raised his head and looked Billy in the eye. "They're dead."

Sonny glanced at Billy and then back at the young man, still crouched over. "You're absolutely sure?" he said.

The young man straightened up and looked at Sonny. "Yeah... We're sure."

Billy asked, "We?"

The young man replied, "My wife and I." Then he pointed to the car parked just a few yards from the spot they were standing. "We hiked up that trail to where it met the Sugarland Mountain Trail, rested a bit, and then decided to walk a little farther up the mountain. We're not hard-core hikers, so we stopped several times. Finally, my wife had to, well, you know..." Both rangers were listening intently, so the young man continued, "...make a nature call. As we walked off the trail out into the woods, she spotted the person."

Sonny asked again, "You're absolutely sure that the individual is deceased?"

The young man rubbed his forehead. "There's no doubt, sir. I've only seen things like that in the movies. I really don't know if my wife will ever go walking in the woods again."

Billy slightly adjusted his head and asked, "Seen what kind of things?"

The young man placed his hand over his heart and answered, "It looks like this person's chest is gone."

Sonny and Billy looked at each other. Both men were well aware that there were plenty of opportunistic animals in the park that could have found this person before the couple did, but whatever had taken place, the rangers knew they were going to need assistance on this one. Sonny helped the young man over to his vehicle, and once there, he noticed the wife sitting in the front seat staring out the windshield. The expression on her face made her appear frozen in time. But it was obvious that the woman was stricken with fear by the quivering of her hands which rested in her lap. Sonny noticed that barely outside the door, the woman had lost whatever she had eaten for breakfast that morning.

When Sonny spoke to the young lady through the partially opened window, she immediately jumped and screamed. Sonny was quick to apologize and tugged on the husband's arm as they moved to the back of the car. Sonny patted the man's shoulder and said, "Try to help her calm down if you can. We're going to call for someone to assist with your wife also."

The man nodded, and Sonny walked back to the ranger truck. Billy was still talking on the radio trying to inform the dispatcher of everybody and everything they needed. Every now and then, Sonny would glance back at the young couple. Each time he did, the young man was kneeling down on one knee at the door, rubbing his wife's arm and staring down at the ground.

Finally, Billy looked over at Sonny while waiting on the dispatcher's response. "What's up?" he asked.

Sonny answered, "We're gonna need another team for the wife. She's shook up pretty bad... maybe in shock."

Billy nodded and then informed the dispatcher about the young man's wife; they acknowledged the request and immediately dispatched another EMT crew. Sonny walked back over to the young couple after retrieving the notebook from the ranger truck. He motioned for the husband to step away from the door for a second and informed him they were sending somebody to assist his wife.

Sonny then took down the couple's information and the tag number of their vehicle. The young man had regained his composure as much as anyone could in a situation like this, and now his conversation with Sonny was much more coherent.

Billy exited the truck and stood beside the road; he deterred any more vehicles from exiting the road into the parking area. He realized that, shortly, they would need all the parking space possible for the emergency vehicles that would be arriving.

Sonny closed the notebook and slid it into the left pocket of his cargo pants, then clipped the pen to the inside of his shirt pocket. He addressed the young man, "They probably will transport your wife to the hospital to be checked out. If there's any way possible... I would like for you to lead us to the body."

The young man glanced at the car and then back at Sonny. "I'll explain to her that you guys need my help. I'll assure her that I will be at the hospital as soon as possible."

Sonny replied, "We would really appreciate it... If you want, I can have someone drive you to the hospital. I can get a tow truck to bring your car there. There won't be any charge. If you can just get us to the right location, it would be a big help."

The young man nodded and walked back to the side of the car. Sonny watched as he explained the details to his wife. At first, Sonny was worried that the conversation was not going well. Then the woman nodded, and the young man leaned in to give her a hug. Sonny let out a long sigh.

Hopefully, the young lady could overcome whatever she had seen out in the woods.

CHAPTER 2

It didn't take long before the first of the emergency responders arrived at the parking area for the hiking trails. Fortunately, the first to pull off the highway was an ambulance with the EMTs to administer care for the young lady in the car. Sonny and Billy were both relieved at the sight of the vehicle. One by one, the emergency personnel arrived and secured a place to park beside the road. Billy continued to assist with the tourist traffic while Sonny ushered the medical team to the car to assist the young man's wife.

After several minutes of controlled chaos, the woman was helped from the car to the ambulance. She received some reassurance from her husband and then a kiss on the forehead. In just a few minutes, the ambulance exited the parking area and sped down the highway toward the hospital. The empty spot was quickly taken by a white SUV with the Medical Examiner logo clearly printed on both sides.

The driver's door opened, and Rhonda Billingsly graciously slid out of the seat and firmly planted both feet onto the ground. Rhonda was a five-foot six-inch blonde attributed with all the athletic features needed to tackle any mountainous hike that the area could offer, which was exactly what she participated in the biggest majority of the time when she was not working.

Rhonda opened the back hatch of the vehicle to grab her gear just as Sonny approached the SUV and asked, "Ready for a little hike, Rhonda?"

"Yeah, buddy... Just wish it was more of a pleasure hike instead of work,"

Rhonda replied as she pulled her backpack out of the back compartment.

Sonny responded, "That makes two of us."

Then Rhonda glanced around the parking lot until she noticed the young man that appeared out of place. "What have we got, Sonny?" she asked.

Sonny looked at the young man still standing beside his car and the ranger that was accompanying him. He said, "The young man and his wife found a deceased individual somewhere beside the Sugarland Mountain Trail. Appears that something has already been... you know, feeding on the remains."

Rhonda raised her eyebrows slightly. "Make sure I get to examine everything thoroughly before someone contaminates the area."

Sonny smiled. "Will do... Ready?"

Sonny and Rhonda walked over to the young man and asked if he was ready to go; he simply nodded yes. Sonny, Rhonda, Billy, the young man, and a small army of first responders crossed the road. The group entered the woods and began the trek up the Husky Gap Trail that intersected the Sugarland Mountain Trail. They walked at a steady pace, taking several breaks to assist the individuals that were carrying the heavier gear. There was almost no conversation between the members of the group until they met the spot where the two trails crossed. Everyone came to a halt to take a breather.

Sonny addressed the young man, "We turn to the left and start up the mountain, right?"

The young man answered, "Yes, sir... I'm not sure how far it is, but I'll recognize it when we get there."

Sonny patted the man's shoulder. "Just take your time, son... When you're ready, we'll let you lead the way."

The young man took a deep breath and began to move up the trail. Sonny fell into line behind him, and the rest of the group followed suit. They would walk for several minutes and then the man would stop to rest, each time surveying the forest around them. Sonny was beginning to wonder if the man would indeed recognize the spot again or not; this might be a little difficult for someone who was not familiar with the area. Most of the visitors that ventured onto one of the many hiking trails of the area could not give an accurate description of the forest around them, especially locating an isolated spot they had been to on the trail.

After covering a small distance from the last resting spot, the young man came to an abrupt stop. After studying the woods for just a couple of seconds, to his right he pointed and said, "It's right over there."

Sonny instructed one of the rangers to stay with the young man, then he informed the group that Rhonda was in charge from that point on. She made her way past Sonny and slowly began traversing the forest, carefully scanning in all directions with her eyes. They had moved about 75 yards from the trail when Rhonda suddenly lifted her arm. The group immediately stopped in their tracks.

Rhonda turned her head to face the group. "I see the victim. Let me go and check it out. You guys keep a good lookout... If something has been feeding on the body, we wouldn't want it to catch us off guard."

Everybody nodded and took a few steps to spread out and guard her as she moved to the body, but nobody moved as much as an inch closer. The last thing that any members of the group desired was to come under the wrath of the Medical Examiner's Office. It only took a few minutes for Rhonda to reach the victim, even though it seemed like an eternity for the others as they watched her study the area with each step she took. Right away, Rhonda noticed there were no drag marks in the leaves, the victim was a male, and he had met his demise in the very spot where he lay. As she examined the man, she noticed that the chest cavity appeared to have been torn apart. Upon further examination, she found that the man's internal organs were missing.

Rhonda took a long, hard look around the body on the forest floor, but other than the red droplets of blood covering the leaves, there were no signs of any part of the internal organs anywhere. After a few more minutes of studying the site carefully, Rhonda asked Sonny and two of the emergency personnel to bring a body bag to place the male victim in.

The three men cautiously approached Rhonda and then asked for instructions. She had them place the bag on the ground beside the victim. As Rhonda and Sonny rolled the individual onto his side to allow the bag to be maneuvered under him, she caught sight of the large gashes in the man's sweatshirt. She paused at the sight of the blood-soaked material and the exposed flesh that appeared to have been sliced deeply with the precision of a sharp knife.

Rhonda looked up at the three men and said, "Let's be really careful, guys." Once the individual was securely in the bag, Rhonda asked the two emergency workers to carry him back to the trail. She then turned to Sonny and said, "Something's wrong here, Sonny."

"What were those gashes in his back, Rhonda?" Sonny asked.

Rhonda took a deep breath. "Not sure, Sonny... We'll have to check him out back at the office. But there's no backpack or even a water bottle. Was he just roaming around out here in the woods or what?"

Sonny replied, "It's a long way up and down this trail, plus there's not another vehicle parked down at the highway."

Rhonda looked out through the forest. "Have everybody spread out and take a look around... If they spot something, have them give us a yell."

Sonny made his way back to the others who remained ever watchful of the surroundings and passed along Rhonda's instructions; everybody slowly spread out and began to search the woods. The group methodically moved between the trees, pausing intermittently to survey the forest in all directions. The sun was beaming through the treetops and colliding with the leaves that covered the forest floor. The fragrance that surrounded the men was pure late spring mountain air. It seemed like just another perfect day in the park—that is, except for the fact that they had just recovered a body and were now looking for anything that might appear odd to Rhonda.

After several minutes, the serenity of the forest was shattered when Billy yelled, "Over here, Chief!"

The rest of the search party stopped and stood steadfast in their positions. Sonny and Rhonda made their way to Billy. He had not moved since the scene first came into view. Directly in front of Billy at about 30 yards was what appeared to be a campsite. The visible bare legs and orange socks protruding from what was left of a tent next to an old fallen log was a sight that Billy could not take his eyes off of. As Sonny and Rhonda came along beside him, he merely pointed at the campsite.

Rhonda asked the men to stay put for a second until she had a look, and neither man spoke as she moved to the site. They watched as she examined the body and then the area around the campsite. Next, Rhonda turned and motioned for the two men to come to her.

When Sonny and Billy entered the campsite, Billy was the first to speak, "Oh my gosh... What happened here?"

Rhonda looked at the two men. "Her internal organs are missing... just like the male victim up there."

Billy glanced at the canvas of the tent. "Look at those gashes in the tent... Were they inside when something attacked?"

Rhonda answered, "I don't think so. The two sleeping bags are still zipped up, and the tent is zipped up also. I think the rips in the tent material and the fact that some of the tent poles are broken is just a product of the violence that occurred here. Look at her face, Sonny. That gash is quite similar to the male victim's back."

"So, you think they were just sitting here by the fire when whatever happened took place?" Billy asked.

Rhonda nodded and said, "There's still some warm embers down in the ashes of the fire... These two individuals were killed last night, probably right after dark."

Sonny stated, "This doesn't add up to be an animal we have in the park, Rhonda... Even her bear spray is still clipped to her shorts."

Rhonda replied, "I think this happened really fast, Sonny. She probably didn't have time to react to the attack. And whatever it was, it scared the male victim so bad he took off running through the darkness of the woods. There was no flashlight near the body... He was running blindly in the night."

Billy knelt beside the woman and said, "Could it possibly have been a big cat? We don't talk about the mountain lions often, but we all know they roam the area. People see them all over the Appalachian Mountains."

Rhonda shrugged her shoulders, "I don't really think so. The gashes don't really match one of the big cat's claws. And off the record, Sonny... I agree with you; this doesn't match any of the animals here in the park. We'll see what these two have to tell us when we get them back to the office."

Rhonda instructed the two men of everything she wanted collected and bagged for the return trip to the Examiner's Office, basically everything but the trees around the campsite. Sonny and Billy called for the others to come over to the campsite. Once there, everybody put on gloves and began to place every item into a bag. All the bags were then sealed and placed in larger bags for transportation. Sonny and Billy assisted Rhonda with placing the second victim into the body bag, and once everything had been collected, the journey back to the Sugarland Mountain Trail began.

Once the team arrived at the trail, the four men standing there realized there was a second victim. When Sonny made eye contact with them, he said, "Apparently these two were camping just off the trail last night. Hopefully, we can determine exactly what happened."

Sonny and Billy were still gripping the nylon handles of the second victim's bag; the other two rangers grabbed the straps for the male victim's bag and lifted it off the ground. Soon the entire group was walking in single file down the mountain trail. Then they took a right turn onto the Husky Gap Trail and started the descent to the parking area. After numerous stops to rest for the personnel carrying the heavier items, they could finally hear the many tourist vehicles going up and coming down the mountain. Two of the rangers stopped the almost continuous flow of traffic in order for the parade of emergency personnel to cross the road.

Once everything was loaded, Rhonda turned to Sonny. "I'll be in touch... When I find out something, you'll be the first to know."

Sonny smiled. "Appreciate it, Rhonda... Get me some good info, okay?"

Rhonda winked at Sonny and climbed into the SUV. As soon as the vehicle was started, she placed it into gear, and the vehicle sped down the road.

Sonny walked over to the young man. "Thanks for all your help," he said. "You need someone to drive you to the hospital?"

The young man replied, "No, sir... I'll be alright."

Sonny shook the man's hand and said, "Hope your wife is okay. If there's anything you need, just let us know."

The young man smiled and nodded, then climbed into his car and left the parking area. Sonny and Billy assisted with the traffic as each of the emergency vehicles vacated the area. In just a matter of a couple minutes, they were the only ones who remained.

The two men walked over to the truck and leaned against the front of it; neither man spoke for several minutes as they ran the day's events through their minds.

Finally, Sonny pushed off the truck and asked, "How about giving me a ride back to the visitor center?"

Billy replied, "You got it, Chief."

CHAPTER 3

Several eyes had been focused on the two victims during the examination of their bodies. Apparently, the condition in which they had been found had been discussed amongst many. Once the bodies had been washed and they lay naked on the examining tables, the wounds were clearly more visible. The gashes in the male and female victims were much larger and deeper than they first appeared. The violence that occurred was astounding, and Rhonda couldn't help but wonder exactly what it was that these people fatefully met in the darkness that night.

The injuries in the chest cavities were something that none of the examiners had ever witnessed before. A closely calculated search into the open wounds on each victim's chest began to reveal even more questions than answers. It appeared that something had penetrated deep into the skin and then ripped the chest of each individual open by pulling in opposite directions. Not only were there precise incisions of the outer skin, but in some places, it had been ripped open by sheer force. The skin had the appearance of being torn like a sheet of paper rather than smoothly cut with a pair of scissors.

The heart, liver, and lungs of both victims were clearly missing. And since they were not at the kill site, it was assumed that something had consumed the organs. As the chest cavities were cleaned, Rhonda took note that the tissue around the area where the organs once were had the same appearance as the outer skin; some areas looked like they had been cut with the precision of a knife, while others were jagged along the edges.

As Rhonda continued to probe, something abruptly caught her attention. Down close to the spine of the male victim was a long black hair lying against the bone. She extracted the hair with a pair of tweezers and immediately placed it into a small evidence bag; next she sealed the bag and placed it on a small rolling tray to her right. As they continued to wash the two victims, the deep gouges and tooth marks became more and more visible on the bones inside each body. Measurements were taken on all the wounds, and countless pictures were taken to document all the damage associated with the bones.

After the examination, the hair was sent to a state lab for identification. Rhonda already had her concerns about the hair. After studying it closely, she had already concluded in her own mind that it definitely didn't belong to one of the black bears of the region. Rhonda just couldn't figure out what exactly the long black hair belonged to. Then Rhonda cleaned up and walked to her office. She closed the door and began to fill out the preliminary report paperwork.

Once she was finished, Rhonda leaned back in the large office chair and placed her hands behind her head. The wounds, the hair, and the condition of the bodies raced through her mind. She really had no explanation for what took place out there in the darkness of the night. Rhonda hoped that the analysis of the hair would shed some light on the situation. She called it a day and left the office to go home, but the drive and the meal Rhonda picked up on the way did very little to clear her mind of the things she had seen.

* * *

Days turned into weeks as Sonny and Billy continued to perform their duties as park rangers, but neither could get the gruesome scene from beside the Sugarland Mountain Trail out of their minds. They only discussed what was discovered out in the forest on that fateful day in private conversation with each other. Neither man had an explanation for what happened to the victims, but both of them wanted answers.

At 15 minutes till eight on Saturday morning, there was a knock at Sonny and Sarah's door, and Sarah slid her chair away from the breakfast table and began to walk through the kitchen. Sarah was wearing the knee-length cotton gown that she had put on the night before. As she passed the coat rack that Sonny had mounted beside the kitchen door, she lifted the robe off the peg and swung it around her body.

Sarah then turned to Sonny, who had stopped eating and was watching her gracefully cross the room. She smiled and said, "Better put this thing on... Wouldn't want someone to go into cardiac arrest when I open the door."

Sonny laughed and responded, "Yeah... Don't know how we would explain that."

Sarah recognized the face outside the door as soon as it became visible through the gap in the curtains of the door window. She unlocked the deadbolt and opened the door. As Billy lifted his head to address her, Sarah asked, "And just what brings you out here on your day off, young man?"

Billy smiled and said, "Is Sonny busy?"

Sarah chuckled and answered, "Busy eating breakfast... Come on in and I'll fix you a plate."

Billy stepped into the chalet and made his way to the small table in the dining room. After closing and locking the door, Sarah followed Billy across the hardwood floors. After entering the kitchen, she opened one of the cabinet doors and retrieved another plate. Then she proceeded to fill the plate with scrambled eggs, two slices of bacon, and the two remaining slices of toast. Sarah placed the plate, along with a coffee cup, down in front of Billy. He smiled again and thanked her as he reached for the coffee pot sitting on the table.

Sonny smiled at Sarah and then asked Billy, "So... What brings you to our neck of the woods on your day off?"

Billy looked at Sarah and then back to Sonny. He said, "That's exactly what Sarah asked me at the door. Can't a guy come to visit his friends?"

Sonny grinned. "I just figured you had already seen enough of me at work. Kinda makes me nervous when you show up at the house unannounced."

Billy laughed and said, "Well, as a matter of fact, I do have something on my mind."

"Now, we are getting somewhere," Sonny said. "What can we help you with?"

Billy sat his fork down, picked up the napkin and wiped his face, then looked Sonny in the eye and said, "I can't get those two people out of my mind... I want to go back up there and look around some more. I was kinda hoping you would go with me."

Sarah was the next to speak, "We would love to, Billy."

Sonny smiled at Sarah. "And what about all those honey-do items you had for me today?"

Sarah shrugged her shoulders, "They can wait." Then she turned to Billy. "I've been trying to get Sonny to take me out there so I can get a glimpse of what is keeping him up at night."

Sonny leaned back in the chair. "I told you about everything we saw out there, honey."

Sarah tilted her head and opened her hands, "I know, Sonny... but maybe it would help to go back and revisit the area."

Billy dropped his eyes to the table. "I'm having trouble sleeping too... Something's not right, Chief. Even Rhonda had her suspicions out in the woods that day. And to top it off, we haven't heard a word from her in person. The preliminary report we got from the Medical Examiner's Office was pretty vague, Chief, not to mention that there was no alert placed in the park for a rogue animal. It was just like... Let's get back to normal and keep rolling along."

Sonny lifted his eyebrows and said, "I really did expect Rhonda to talk to us personally. Maybe another look is in order."

30 minutes later, Sonny and Sarah climbed into Billy's truck, and the three pulled out of the driveway and started down the road. The morning sun was trying to penetrate the fog that had developed on the mountains the night before, but there were only limited areas where it was succeeding. The fog wasn't so thick that one couldn't see to drive, but just dense enough to make it impossible to see very far into the forest.

As Billy navigated the curvy road, he and Sonny continued to discuss that fateful day, everything from the moment the man flagged them down until the bodies were returned to the parking area. Sarah sat behind the men, taking in each and every word of their conversation. She had been totally intrigued with that day's events ever since Sonny had shared them with her at the dinner table that night. Usually, Sonny only mentioned the unique things that occurred while he was at work, and this was without a doubt the most unique thing he had ever mentioned.

Finally, Billy turned on the signal to enter the parking area, and all three were quick to notice there was already a vehicle parked in one of the spots. Billy pulled his pickup truck up beside the parked jeep and turned to Sonny. "Early hikers, I guess," he said.

Sonny responded, "Yeah... and they have no idea what occurred here several weeks ago."

The three of them placed their day hiking packs on, grabbed their walking sticks, and crossed the road, and within a matter of seconds they started the walk up the Husky Gap Trail.

The trek with the emergency personnel and the young man on that fateful day ran through the minds of both men as they continued the slow, steady pace up the trail. After just a few stops to rest, the trio came to the intersection of the Sugarland Mountain Trail. As they stopped, Sonny leaned against a large tree and stared up at the mountain.

Sonny turned his head and faced Billy. "When we were going up this trail, I wasn't totally sure that the young man was going to get us to the right spot."

Billy smiled. "Yeah... I kinda had my doubts too. I figured we were in for a pretty big search grid."

Sonny nodded and said, "I have to admit, though, he was spot on when he stopped and pointed out into the forest."

Sarah interrupted, "Okay, boys... That's enough chit-chat. Let's go a little farther."

Sonny shook his head and said to Billy, "Maybe we should have left her at the house."

Billy laughed, "Oh no, Chief, you're not gonna get me into trouble... She fed me breakfast this morning."

Sarah laughed and said, "Come on, boys... Let's move up the trail."

The three continued to move at a steady pace, observing all that was happening around them. The native birds were darting from tree limb to tree limb. There was a mother deer and her newborn fawn, still covered in spots, slowly ambling beside the trail just in front of the group. The little fawn was intrigued with the three strange visitors to its home; it would take a few steps then turn its head to take a look at the trio, then repeat the process, staying ever close to the mother deer. The older deer was already accustomed to seeing humans due to the many visitors to the park. Squirrels raced across the leaves and played their games in the trees.

Sonny came to a stop and turned to the others, "Well... Here we are, people."

Sarah took a deep breath. "Lead the way, Mr. Park Ranger."

Billy snickered and said, "Yeah, Chief... Lead the way."

Sonny just rolled his eyes. "You people."

Sarah laughed as Sonny turned and began to lead the group through the trees. Everybody was walking as though they were trying to sneak up on something out in the forest. None of them knew why they were acting in this manner; for some unknown reason, it just seemed to fit the situation. Suddenly Sonny came to a stop and held out his hand, and Sarah and Billy leaned out their heads to get a clear look beyond Sonny's position. There was a lone individual down on their hands and knees scouring the forest floor. The person was totally oblivious to the fact that they were being watched by the trio.

After studying the individual for several minutes, Sonny recognized the person. He turned to Sarah and Billy. "That's Rhonda... Wonder what she's up to?"

Billy whispered, "Let's go have a look."

They made their way closer to Rhonda, who still had no earthly idea that anyone was close by. Finally, Sonny said, "Rhonda."

Rhonda gasped loudly as she wheeled around. She placed her hand against her chest and said, "Good gosh, Sonny... You almost gave me a heart attack."

Sonny asked, "What are you looking for?"

Rhonda glanced at all three and then answered, "Let's talk a minute... off the record, okay?"

Sonny tilted his head, "Another 'off the record,' huh?"

Rhonda smiled. "Yep."

The three of them walked up to Rhonda, who was still sitting in the leaves. They all grabbed a nice hard seat on an old fallen log facing her and said they were all ears. Next, Rhonda divulged the details of the examination of the bodies that she had concerns about. She described the hair that was extracted from the male victim's chest cavity.

Rhonda looked Sonny in the eyes. "The hair came back as unknown, but it more than likely belonged to a bear or wolf."

Billy spoke next, "There's quite a bit of DNA difference between a bear and a wolf."

Rhonda shook her head yes. "Exactly... and the hair was in really good shape. There shouldn't be a problem with identification, but for some reason, the state lab did not return the hair. I don't think they know exactly what the hair belongs to, so... I'm out here looking for a needle in a haystack."

Sarah came to her feet and said, "So... you need another hair."

Rhonda replied, "Yes. If I can find one, I have a friend that owes me a favor."

Billy asked, "What about the campsite?"

Rhonda answered, "I'm not having any luck here at the male victim's location. Maybe four sets of eyes can turn up something there."

The next three hours were spent meticulously searching the ground at the campsite, but nothing stood out as the four people crawled around on the ground. Sarah rolled off her hands and knees and came to rest on her rearend against a large, moss-covered log. Next, she rubbed her eyes as she arched her back to stretch out the tired muscles of her body. Just as Sarah's vision cleared, she spotted the small, thin object clinging to the broken limb of a small sapling.

Sarah smiled and said, "Rhonda... I think right there is what we are looking for."

Rhonda came to her feet and made her way to Sarah. Then Sarah pushed off the log and stood beside Rhonda and pointed. "There, at the break in the limb."

Rhonda studied the hair closely, then removed it with a pair of tweezers and placed it in an evidence bag. Rhonda turned to the others and said, "I think we got it, people. Way to go, Sarah."

The four people made their way back down to the parking area, and Rhonda asked them not to disclose to anyone what they had found. She promised that as soon as she had some information, they would all get together to discuss the findings of the hair. Everyone agreed to keep the secret, and soon all were heading back down the road.

CHAPTER 4

It was just after midnight and there wasn't a cloud in the night sky. The full moon was reflecting off the calm waters of the lake. It looked like a person could easily count a million stars glistening up above. Ronnie and Steve had been fishing for several hours now after unloading the boat at the ramp and making the trip down to their favorite part of the lake. South Holston Reservoir is a mountainous lake situated in upper East Tennessee and Southwest Virginia. For both men, this was definitely one of their favorite lakes to fish in.

It was Friday night, and the usual fishing tournament was in full swing, but Ronnie and Steve had the area they were fishing in almost completely to themselves. There was only one other boat sharing the long hollow with its many secondary points diving into the lake and disappearing below the water's edge. As the two men fished along, they talked about how nice it was to finally reach retirement age. Now in life, about the only thing that regulated their outings to the lake was the weather.

Just as they were beginning to move around the point they were fishing, Ronnie felt the small tug on the plastic worm he was slowly bouncing off the shale rock that made up the lake bottom. He arched his back and jerked the fishing rod in an upward direction; immediately Ronnie felt the fish begin its fight to free itself of the hook. Suddenly the smooth water erupted as the smallmouth bass made the first of several leaps. By the sound of the splash and the ripples created, Ronnie knew it was a good one.

Steve grabbed the net and joined Ronnie at the front of the boat, and soon the two men had the lunker fish in the boat and were enjoying the success of their teamwork. After removing the hook and studying the fish for just a few seconds, Ronnie gently placed it back in the water, and the fish swished its tail on the surface and disappeared into the darkness of the lake.

Steve returned the net to its proper place in hopes they would need it again and it could be located quickly at a moment's notice. As he returned to the rear of the craft, Steve found his fishing rod and turned to face the bank. The boat had drifted far enough out in front of the point to see the next areas for the men to attack with their lures.

That's when Steve noticed another boat ahead of them floating in the middle of the cove. He glanced at Ronnie and said, "Hey, Ronnie... Looks like someone else likes this spot."

Ronnie looked off the bow of the boat and responded, "Maybe it's one of the tournament boats... Wonder why he's floating in the middle of the cove?"

Then Ronnie chuckled, "I'll bet they've caught so many, they're having to take a breather."

Steve's belly shook as he laughed, "Yeah... I bet so. But we can still fish up this side and not get in their way."

Ronnie took another quick glance in the direction of the boat and then returned to focusing on the task at hand. "I reckon so. We'll fish along the left bank and try not to intrude on them."

The two men continued to fish and were lucky enough to boat a couple more bass. Both would periodically look at the boat ahead, but neither saw anyone nor heard any type of conversation from that direction. The boat and the entire area surrounding it was eerily quiet. As they got closer, Ronnie stopped his pursuit of another catch and took another long, hard look at the craft as it sat silently on the water.

Finally, Ronnie broke the silence of the night, "Hey... You guys okay?"

There was no response, so Steve whispered, "Ronnie... Something's not right."

What the men heard next sent chills down their spines. Ronnie turned to Steve and asked, "You hear that?"

Steve answered, "Yes, I did... Sounds like whimpering."

This time, Ronnie spoke a little louder, "You guys okay?"

All the two men could hear were the muffled sounds of something coming from the boat, almost like the sounds of someone crying but at a very low, terrified tone. Steve grabbed the spotlight and aimed it at the boat. When he flicked the switch on, not only were the navigation lights visible, but the entire boat was illuminated. The boat appeared to be empty, but the muffled sounds continued to travel in Ronnie and Steve's direction. Ronnie adjusted the trolling motor and pressed the on switch with his foot, and the prop of the electric motor came to life. The two men watched as they closed in on the seemingly empty boat.

The sound became louder and louder as they drew closer to the vessel until the men were directly alongside of the boat. Ronnie and Steve stood speechless as they focused on the woman sitting on the floor, almost in a fetal position. Her face was hidden against her knees with the woman's arms wrapped around her legs; she had no idea that the two men were even staring at her.

Steve leaned over and placed both hands on the boat to keep them close. Ronnie carefully stepped into her boat and touched her shoulder as he spoke, "Ma'am, are you alright?"

The woman's scream echoed across the lake as she started flailing her arms and kicking her legs. Ronnie tried to reassure the lady, "It's okay... It's okay. We'll help you, honey... It's okay."

The woman quit swinging her arms and wrapped them around Ronnie. Her eyes were looking in every direction in a frantic display of fear but weren't focusing on any particular object. Even though the lady's arms were tightly wrapped around Ronnie, her body was shaking uncontrollably. Ronnie tried to reassure the woman again, but nothing seemed to help. Steve removed his hoodie sweatshirt and gave it to Ronnie to place around the woman.

Next, Steve opened one of the many storage compartments of Ronnie's boat and found his cellphone in the bag of extra clothes he had brought for the trip. When he pressed the button, Steve was elated to see the signal bars on the lighted screen. Immediately, he dialed 911 and waited for a response. It only took one ring before the dispatcher began to speak.

"911, what's your emergency?" the voice asked.

Steve answered, "This is Steve Hensley... My buddy and I are fishing on South Holston Lake. We have found a woman floating in a boat, and she appears to be in shock. We're not sure what has happened, but we need some assistance."

The dispatcher began to ask a series of questions, some of which didn't seem to have any significance to the situation at hand. But nonetheless, Steve answered each and every one. After just a minute, the dispatcher paused and Steve grabbed the opportunity to say, "Please hurry and get us some help out here."

The dispatcher assured Steve that the correct people would be on their way very shortly and asked him for their exact location. They instructed the two men to remain with the woman until the authorities arrived, then the phone went silent as the dispatcher began to contact and organize the assistance needed.

Steve placed the small device in his pocket and turned to Ronnie, who was still holding the lady, and said sarcastically, "Surely she didn't think we were just gonna leave her and go back to fishing."

Ronnie replied, "I don't think so, Steve... but that was a kinda odd thing to say."

Ronnie gently positioned the woman and sat her in one of the boat's seats, then he slowly sat beside her and repositioned the sweatshirt in an effort to cover her upper body. Steve rummaged through the boat's compartments until he located a jacket to place over the woman's legs. He leaned over the edge of the boat and helped Ronnie cover them in an effort to keep her warm. She was still shaking but seemed to calm somewhat.

Ronnie whispered to the lady, "Honey... What happened?"

Just as he finished, there was a long, lonely howl that emerged from somewhere on the mountain behind them that echoed softly through the network of lake hollows. The sound seemed to gently roll past them and diminish as it made its way toward the dam. Steve raised his head and stared in the direction of the howl on the mountain. The woman began to shake uncontrollably, and she jerked her head in all directions. Ronnie tightened his grip on the woman to try to reassure her that they were there, and everything was going to be okay. It took several minutes for her to calm down, but her trembling never stopped. Steve wanted to question Ronnie about the howl but dared not mention it after he witnessed the effect it had on the woman.

* * *

Tennessee Wildlife and Resource Agency Officer Joseph Wales sat straight up in bed as the phone began to ring. After locating just exactly where the annoying tone was coming from, he pushed the answer softkey on the screen of the device. The voice emerging from inside the cellphone gave Joseph the details of the emergency. Next, he was informed that his partner, Phillip, had already been notified and would meet him at the marina.

After donning his TWRA uniform, Joseph leaned over and kissed his wife on the forehead. He whispered, "I'll see you when I get back, honey."

Joe's wife replied, "Happy trails... Be careful, Joe."

Joe started the TWRA pickup truck and removed his cellphone from his shirt pocket. He dialed Phillip's number and waited. Just two rings and

Phillip answered, “Yeah, Joe... I’m up and pulling out of the driveway.”

Joe laughed and said, “Yeah, me too... Did you get a good explanation of what we are heading into?”

Phillip answered, “Just that a couple of fishermen found a woman floating in a boat all alone, and she appeared to be in shock.”

Joe said, “Sounds like the story I got, too... I’ll see you at the dock.”

Both men pressed the “end call” button on their phones, exited their driveways, and sped down the road. Traffic was at a minimum, so navigating the roads to the lake was no problem at all. Joe kept thinking of how nice it would be to have his coffee, but there wasn’t sufficient time to prepare it. He would just have to do without for now, but just maybe the marina would have a fresh pot on at daybreak. Joe had all the confidence in the world that they would probably get to view the sunrise from the agency’s boat.

Phillip was the first to arrive at the marina next to the Route 421 bridge that crossed the lake. After parking his vehicle, Phillip switched on his flashlight and walked down to the ramp that traversed from the solid ground to the floating structures that made up the marina. He could see the numerous lights from all the structures reflecting on the water of the lake as he got to the aluminum ramp. Phillip abruptly stopped and turned as he heard the truck pulling into the parking lot. He politely waited on Joe to catch up to him at the ramp and then said, “I was hoping not to see you for a few more hours, Joe. At least not till morning.”

Joe smiled and replied, “Well technically... We are on the AM side of the clock, Phil.”

Phil shook his head. “I kinda meant when the sun was shining, Joe. I wonder what this is all about?”

Joe replied, “Not sure... but the dispatcher said the guy that called it in was pretty shaken up.”

The two crossed the ramp and walked onto the platform that supported the main building of the marina. The creaking sound emitting from the dock as they walked to the TWRA boat echoed across the cove. Phil observed the eerie noise and said, "You really don't pay much attention to that noise until everything's really quiet out here."

Joe chuckled, "Yeah... almost like an old scary movie."

Phil grimaced even though Joe was in front and could not see his face. "I hate scary movies, and people do the dumbest things at the dumbest times in those movies."

Joe chuckled, "Well... I don't think the boogeyman is here at the marina. Unless he might be hiding in our boat in the dark."

Phil grunted as they approached the boat, "Very funny, Joe."

Joe stepped off the dock and into the boat. He turned to Phil, who was scanning the interior of the craft with his flashlight. "What are you looking for?" Joe asked.

Phil answered with a grin, "Just checking."

As Joe fired the engine, he nodded to Phil, "Untie us, partner, and let's see what this is all about."

Phil untied the ropes and gave the boat a push out of the slip before hopping in, and both men secured their life vests as the craft floated gently away from the dock. Joe placed the lever in the forward position and idled the craft beyond the "NO WAKE" buoys on the outskirts of the marina. Next, he switched on the blue lights just seconds before pushing the throttle forward to speed down the lake. There were a couple of boats visible along the banks as the two officers rushed down the open corridor toward the dam. The officers turned left just as Cliff Island came into view under the light of the full moon. The lights of the dam were visible beyond the island, which had become a popular place for people to jump off, not only for the thrill of the jump but for the refreshing cooldown from the summer heat as they impacted the water.

After passing Boy Scout Island, the two men could see the Point 3 reflective sign with the aid of their spotlight just ahead. Then they took another left to enter the network of hollows that made up this portion of the lake. Joe eased back on the throttle and brought the boat to an idle, and both men began to scan the area, hoping to locate exactly where the emergency was. Suddenly, just to the right, a spotlight began to signal the officers. Steve had been waiting for what seemed to be an eternity for help to arrive. As soon as he saw the flashing blue lights, Steve started signaling the TWRA boat.

Joe once again pushed the throttle of the boat and started to close in on the flashing white spotlight. Once Steve recognized that they had been spotted, he lay down the light. As they got closer, Joe slowed the boat and eased up to the three people floating in the two boats. Immediately, Joe and Phil noticed one of the men holding the woman sitting with her head hanging down.

Both officers saw the woman trembling uncontrollably with her hands in her lap.

CHAPTER 5

Phil leaned over, then placed both hands on the side of the boat where Ronnie and the woman were sitting. Steve was still holding their boat close on the opposite side. As Phil raised his head to make eye contact with Steve, the lady could clearly be heard taking rapid short breaths. Steve merely placed his hands out in front of himself, tilted his head to the left, and shrugged his shoulders as his eyes met the TWRA officers'.

Joe carefully stepped from the agency's boat onto the front deck of the woman's boat with the aid of his flashlight. Immediately he took note of the two fishing rods lying silently on the carpet on the outer edge of the deck. Slowly, he approached Ronnie and the lady, then he stepped down into the center section of the boat and sat on the deck surface facing the two of them. Joe leaned over and asked the woman, "Honey... Can you tell us what happened?"

There was no response from the woman, so Joe gently touched her shoulder and was about to ask again, when she jerked and began to shake uncontrollably once more. She started flailing her arms around like she was trying to fight something off her. Ronnie tightened his grip on the lady and began to reassure her the best he could. Joe immediately retracted his hand and tried to apologize to the woman, and Ronnie continued to speak to the lady in a soft tone in an effort to calm her. It took a couple of minutes, but finally the lady calmed just enough for Ronnie to loosen the grip his arms had on her. Soon, she was back to the state of just trembling and taking the short rapid breaths.

Joe made his way back to the agency's boat, turned to Phil, and said, "Let's get some help out here. Call for an ambulance and some deputies from the county to meet us at the boat ramp by the bridge."

Joe looked at Ronnie to ask, "Can you help me get her to the ramp?" Ronnie nodded yes, then Joe turned back to Phil and said, "You and the other gentleman stay here until we get back with help. Then we'll try and sort this thing out."

Phil grabbed the radio and began the task of arranging for the necessary assistance that they required. Ronnie explained to the woman about getting her to the ramp so she could be taken to the hospital for medical attention. Joe was only hearing part of the conversation that Phil was having with the dispatcher; he was more concerned with the woman's reaction to Ronnie's explanation of the events that were fixing to take place. Suddenly to everyone's surprise, the lady actually nodded her head in approval. For the first time since they discovered her, Ronnie sensed a moment of relief in the situation.

Within a few minutes, Ronnie and Joe had safely transferred the woman to the other boat and placed her safely in a seat. The men did not attempt to place a life jacket on her; they decided not to push their luck any more than they had to. Phil moved back to the woman's boat and pushed the three people clear; Joe started the outboard motor and idled away from Steve and Phil in the cove.

Once the agency boat was clear, Joe pushed the throttle forward, and the roar of the motor came to life. They were on their way to the boat ramp. Joe and Ronnie both hoped that the transfer from the boat to the ambulance would go smoothly. In just a short time, they would have their answer.

Phil began to search the woman's boat with his flashlight, hoping that something would stand out to provide some answers as to what had scared her so badly. Phil never removed his eyes from what the light was illuminating as he asked Steve to repeat the events that led up to the 911 call. Steve started from the moment they spotted the woman's boat and explained all that had taken place, right up till the moment they saw the flashing blue lights on the officer's boat. As Phil continued to search, Steve suddenly remembered the howl and the adverse effect it had on the woman.

Steve added, "Oh yeah... There's another strange thing that happened."

Phil stopped searching and looked at Steve, "What's that?"

Steve answered, "Well... Ronnie had somewhat gotten the woman to kinda calm down, and then we heard this howl emerging from somewhere up on the mountain. I mean... it was strange. I've never heard anything like it before. But anyway... As soon as it made its way to us here on the water, the woman came unglued. She was already pretty shaken up, but that sound caused her to almost start fighting Ronnie. Just like when your buddy touched her shoulder... That sound really scared her to death."

Phil asked, "What did the howl sound like?"

Steve shook his head and answered, "I don't know how to explain it... It was a long, drawn-out, lonely howl. Almost like the howl of a wolf... You know, like the ones you hear on the television in those animal documentaries."

Phil asked, "And she reacted to it?"

Steve's voice elevated a little, "You bet. She went berserk."

Then Phil shined the light on the floor below the steering wheel. "She wasn't the only one on this boat—at least, not the entire time tonight."

Steve focused on the spot where the officer's light was shining, then Phil added, "Looks like she may have been relaxing and reading a book."

Then the officer shifted the light's beam, and an object came into view. "She was probably using this portable clip-on light to see the pages."

Steve looked at the light lying on the floor underneath the console and the two AA batteries used to power it resting against the side of the support for the console. Steve looked at Phil and asked, "Then where is this other person?"

Phil turned to the front of the boat. "That's the million-dollar question, isn't it?"

Phil stepped onto the forward fishing deck and began to scan that area of the boat. "There's two fishing rods lying here, and the trolling motor is in the water. Somebody was up here fishing while she was reading her book."

Steve tried to follow the light as Phil continued to search the boat, but it was difficult from his point of view. Suddenly Phil froze in his position. He turned to Steve and asked, "Did you notice if the lady was bleeding?"

Steve answered, "Not that I noticed... Why?"

Phil responded, "There's drops of blood on the bow and where the carpet meets the fiberglass." The boat's fiberglass was a light silver metalflake color, which made the red spots easy to distinguish at a glance. Then Phil said, "What in the world done that?"

Steve was about to ask Phil what he was looking at when the officer continued, "There are some really deep scratches in the bow of the boat, and they look really fresh."

Next, Phil noticed the small broken twigs lying on the carpet around the case that held the foot pedal control for the fishing motor. He raised his light and began to scan the shoreline. There were the usual fallen trees angling down the bank and disappearing into the water. The majority of the shale rock bank along with the light-colored soil was quite visible in the officer's light. Steve saw the object trapped in the limbs of a large bush at exactly the same time as Phil.

The light remained on the object as Steve announced, "That's a baseball cap."

Phil exclaimed, "Yes, it is! When the others get back, I believe that's where we need to start."

As the boat ramp at the bridge came into view, Joe spotted the flashing lights of the emergency vehicles, and he felt a small sigh of relief knowing that soon the woman would be on her way to the local hospital for the help she needed. It only took a few more minutes until Joe eased back on the throttle and idled up to the boat slip secured to the shoreline. Joe, Ronnie, and the EMTs successfully transferred the woman from the boat to the waiting ambulance.

After some reassuring from Ronnie, the vehicle's door closed, and it began to exit the parking area. Both Ronnie and Joe were thankful for the smooth transition. The men watched as the flashing lights made their way to the highway. Then the vehicle's siren began to pierce the early morning silence. Everybody watched as the ambulance crossed the bridge and disappeared on the other side of the lake.

Joe turned to the two deputies that were waiting patiently behind them and asked, "You guys ready for a little boat ride?"

The first deputy was a slender man in his early 40s named Nathan. He nodded yes and replied, "I reckon so... What do we have?"

Joe responded, "We're not sure. This man and his fishing partner found her floating in a boat alone in a state of shock."

As he pointed to Ronnie, Joe added, "Both these guys have been really helpful, but I'm sure they would like to go home. So, when we get back to the site, we'll let them leave and the four of us will try and figure out what happened."

Tom, the second deputy who was in his late 20s and just a little heavier than Nathan, asked, "Four?"

Joe answered, "Yeah, my partner is down at the cove with the other fisherman."

The four men walked down to the boat slip and one by one climbed into the TWRA boat. Joe opened a storage area and retrieved two more life jackets for the deputies. They were still securing them when Ronnie untied the boat and pushed them away from the slip, and since they were the only ones there, Joe never bothered to heed the "NO WAKE" buoy out in front of the ramp. Instead, he shoved the throttle forward, and the bow of the boat rose sharply in front of them. In just a couple of seconds, the boat leveled back out and the four men were quickly in route to the cove. Both deputies hoped that Joe had a real good sense of running down the lake in the dark. Just as the four men rounded the point to enter the matrix of coves, daybreak was starting to invade the lake. Joe could see the boats that Steve and Phil were waiting in. The vessels sat eerily on the water as the sky over the mountain began to get the morning glow of the sun.

Once Joe eased up to the boats, greetings were exchanged, and Ronnie was able to board his boat for the first time in a while. Joe thanked the men, then the officers wrote down their addresses and phone numbers. Ronnie and Steve told the officers that if there was anything they needed, to call, and within a few minutes, the boat disappeared from sight as they headed home.

Joe turned to Phil and asked, "Found anything yet?"

Phil nodded and answered, "Well... I don't think she was alone in this boat." Even though the morning light was beginning to slowly replace the darkness, Phil still used his flashlight to highlight the things he began to tell the other three. He continued, "There's a book on the floor and a battery powered light she was probably reading by. There's a couple of fishing rods on the deck... and there are drops of blood on the carpet as well as on the bow of the boat."

Joe and the deputies switched on their flashlights and aimed them at the bow, then Phil continued, "There's a couple of broken twigs lying on the carpet, and take a look at the scratches in the fiberglass of the bow." All three men were confirming everything that Phil was saying with their own lights. Phil stated, "Something happened at the front of this boat, Joe."

Phil shined his light toward the large bush on the bank at the water's edge and said, "And whatever it was... right there is probably where it happened."

Even though the transition from night to daylight made it difficult to see, the red baseball cap was still quite visible with all four flashlights beaming in that direction. Phil climbed over into the boat with the other officers; they tied a rope to the woman's boat and secured it to the TWRA vessel. Joe started the boat, and the men eased over to the shoreline right in front of the bush. The men studied the bank and the water's edge all around the bush.

Something protruding from the water's edge caught one of the deputy's eyes. Nathan pointed and said, "There's the tip of a fishing rod."

The officers inched closer, and it became clear as they studied the object. Joe turned to Nathan and said, "Good eye."

The rest of the fishing rod and reel was clearly visible below the surface of the crystal-clear water as the men aimed their flashlights down into the lake. Phil lifted his light and noticed the freshly broken limbs of the bush. "This is where the twigs in the boat probably came from," he said, "especially since the hat is caught in the branches."

All the men took another look at the red baseball cap suspended in the thick branches of the bush; Tom turned to the right and began to stare at the area of the bank adjacent to the bush. Nathan noticed the puzzled expression on his face. He asked Tom, "What's the matter?"

Tom's eyes never left the shoreline. "Something's been dragged up the bank."

The other three men immediately turned their attention to the area that Tom was staring at. It only took a second for all of them to confirm in their minds that he was indeed correct. The soft soil that accompanied the shale rocks had deep impressions from something heavy, almost like the footprints of a man walking along the bank of the lake. But these were different; the impressions didn't match any human prints that any of the officers had ever witnessed. There were indeed slide marks in the soft bank that clearly indicated that something had been dragged up into the woods where the lake bank ended.

Finally, Deputy Nathan broke the silence, "So... are we saying that something snatched this person out of the front of the boat and then had the strength to just drag him up into the woods? I mean, boys, this bank is pretty steep."

Joe answered, "Strength is an understatement... but everything points to that conclusion."

An eerie silence filled the area as the four men cautiously stared into the trees above the shoreline. The only sound that could be heard was the chirping of the small birds that inhabited the forest around them. Daybreak was now in full swing of taking over the lake. One could see the smooth water stretching all the way to the main channel, but the visibility into the woods beyond a few feet was still nearly impossible.

Joe began to give the layout of the plan ahead, "Phil, we'll pull the boat onto the bank over there. That way, we don't disturb the scene. You get on the radio and get us some more assistance. The three of us will take a look up in the woods, and you guard the boats. Try to keep anyone from entering the cove."

Phil nodded and replied, "I'll float back out in the cove. The blue lights should keep anybody from entering."

Joe turned to the two deputies and asked, "Ready, guys?"

The deputies nodded yes. Phil began to maneuver the boat to the designated landing area. Once there, the craft slid gently onto the soft soil. Joe and the deputies exited the vessel, and Deputy Nathan pushed the boat off the bank. Phil wished them luck, and the three men began to climb the bank that led them into the trees.

CHAPTER 6

Joe and the deputies entered the tree line and slowly began to angle up the ridgeline, trying to intercept the spot where they had all seen the drag marks along the shore. All the men could hear Phil talking on the radio in his attempt to have more help sent their way. Other than Phil's voice and the morning chirping of the native birds, the forest seemed eerily quiet; the youngest deputy, Tom, was more concerned with what might be lying in wait for them than actually trying to find evidence in the leaves.

Suddenly, a loud noise of rustling leaves and the thumping sound of something running caught everyone's attention. Nathan's feet slipped as he turned to look up on the ridge. Just as his knees firmly planted onto the forest floor, he could plainly see the deer rushing up the mountain in an effort to escape the three intruders that had just invaded the forest. Nathan took a deep breath and turned to Tom, who had already drawn his pistol and was standing in a ready-to-fire position.

Nathan smiled and said, "Easy there, young lad... Just a deer."

Tom shook his head and grinned, "I already don't like this situation. You need a hand, old man?"

Joe chuckled lightly and said, "Oh... to be young, Nathan. At least one of us was quick enough to defend our position."

Tom looked around and then back to the other two. "Glad nobody is wearing a body cam. Wouldn't want that footage to get leaked out."

As Nathan placed his hands onto the leaves to push himself up, Tom slid a hand under his arm, and both men slightly grunted as Nathan came back to a standing position. Nathan tilted his head to Tom, then he smiled and nodded in a gesture of appreciation. Soon the three men were once again maneuvering between the trees and over the fallen logs. As they approached the largest downed tree they had encountered so far, Joe paused. He leaned his rearend against the log and swung his left leg across. Some of the moss on what had once been a mighty oak tree was pushed off the bark. When Joe's shoe impacted it, the moss fell harmlessly onto the leaves.

Just as Joe swung his right leg over the tree, he saw what they had been searching for. He pointed and said, "Whatever got dragged up that lake bank, it was dragged through here also."

Deputy Nathan peered around Joe and studied the forest floor; the morning light had become sufficient to see the entire area around them. As Nathan continued to study the marks in the leaves, he said, "They're going to the top of the ridge."

Joe and Tom followed the marks with their eyes, then Tom stated, "Gotta be pretty strong to drag something up that hill… especially something as heavy as a man."

Nathan interjected, "We're still not sure if it was a man, Tom."

Tom never took his eyes off the top of the ridge, "Well, that guy on the front of the boat went somewhere." Then Tom turned to face Joe and Nathan and asked, "What snatches a guy off a boat, then drags him up into the woods?"

Neither man had an answer for Tom. Joe pushed off the log and said, "Let's follow the trail."

Nathan and Tom maneuvered over the old oak log. Then the men slowly made their way to the drag marks. They kept a few feet to the left of the drag area so as not to contaminate any evidence. It was much more difficult now as the men followed the trail, since it was leading them straight up the ridge.

There was no angling out the incline now; it was merely heading up the steep hill toward the top of the ridge. Every few feet, the men would stop to catch their breath for just a couple of minutes, then they would resume the quest at hand.

About halfway up the hill, Joe held out his hand to once again take a break. As he placed his hand on a knee for support, Joe noticed the red substance smeared onto the leaves. He turned his head and said, "Looks like we got blood on the leaves."

Nathan and Tom focused on the spot that Joe was pointing at, then Nathan stated, "That would be my guess too."

Joe picked up a stick and adjusted the leaves. Immediately, the men saw the blood on the dirt. Joe looked up the hill and said, "I'm not sure what we are going to find up there, guys."

Tom replied, "Me neither... but I don't believe it's gonna be good."

It took a couple more rest stops, but the adrenalin of the men had aided them in the last push up the hill. As they reached the top of the ridge, one could see the water of the cove on the other side, but only in the spots that the leaves of the trees allowed. The three men stood silently as they regained their composure from the climb. Joe removed his radio from the carrying case and pressed the transmit key. He asked, "Phil, this is Joe... You got me, buddy?"

Phil was sitting in the boat staring at the hillside that the three men had disappeared into just earlier. When the radio came to life, he jumped to his feet and grabbed the device. Phil pushed the button and answered, "Loud and clear, Joe. Anything yet?"

Joe responded, "We've followed the drag marks to the top of the ridge. Looks like they are heading away from the lake. We are gonna keep following to see if we can find anything. Did you get ahold of some more assistance?"

Phil answered, "Yeah... We got some more agents and deputies on the way. Give me a call if you need anything... Be careful."

Joe responded, "Will do... Out."

As Joe replaced the radio into its case, the deputies arose from the log they were resting on. The men started following the drag marks in the leaves once again. They were only about 50 yards from their last position when Joe suddenly stopped.

White sneakers were clearly visible as they protruded from the base of an old stump. The rest of the fallen tree was blocking what lay above the shoes.

The other two men stepped alongside of Joe and stared at the shoes. Tom drew his pistol again with his right hand. Next, he placed his left hand in the position to support the firing of the weapon, but for now, Tom kept the pistol aimed at the forest floor. The men walked side by side, moving as quietly as they could as they approached the shoes. As they cleared the stump that once supported the fallen tree, the entire scene came into view. The victim was lying flat on his back, staring directly toward the sky.

The tennis shoes were soiled where they had slid along the dirt; the pants were ripped in several places where they had obviously snagged on something coming up the hill. The man's long-sleeved T-shirt was ripped open; only the sleeves that covered his arms remained intact. The victim's throat had two massive gashes, one on each side of the neck. Blood was splattered on the man's face as well as in his blond hair, and his chest was torn apart and gaping open. The forest floor around the body was covered in blood.

Joe stepped over beside the man, careful not to disturb the scene. He peered into the empty chest of the victim. Tom whispered, "I think we can now say it *was* a person being dragged up that hill."

Nathan replied, "Yeah... we're sure now."

Tom turned and took a few steps away; he took a deep breath and scanned the woods. Joe lifted his eyes and looked at Nathan, then said, "His organs are gone."

Tom wheeled around. "What?"

Joe answered, "His internal organs are missing."

"Something eat them?" Tom asked.

Joe and Nathan took a good look around the area, then Joe responded, "I don't know... They're not in his chest cavity, and I don't see them lying on the ground."

Tom sighed and questioned the men, "Okay, once again... What rips a man out of his boat and drags him through the woods? Not only through the woods, but up a steep hillside that's almost impossible to climb, and consumes his organs?"

Nathan placed his hand on the back of his head and said, "Something pretty strong... and something evil."

The sun was now peeking over the Holston Mountain Range and beginning to shine its rays between the trees of the ridge. The men heard boat motors running in the direction of the cove below them. Joe unsnapped the case and removed the radio. He keyed the device and said, "Phil, is that our help arriving?"

Phil responded, "Yes, sir... They'll be here in just a minute. They just spotted me and are heading this way."

Joe replied back, "Better make another call... We need a medical examiner. We got a body."

Phil took another look toward the ridge and answered, "Roger that."

Joe pressed the button again. "I'm gonna send one of the deputies back down. He can lead a couple more people up here to secure the area. When the examiner gets here, we'll just repeat the process. And Phil...Block off the entire cove; we don't want anyone disturbing the area."

Phil responded, "Gotcha, Joe."

Joe put the radio into its case on his belt, then turned to the deputies and asked, "Who would like to volunteer for the escort of our new arrivals?"

Tom finally returned his firearm to its holster and responded, "That would be me, Joe... Wouldn't want old Nathan making that trek again."

Nathan grinned. "Appreciate that, Mr. Tom."

Tom turned and began the walk back down to the lake; Nathan found a comfortable seat on an old log facing up the ridge. Joe backed up several feet and found him a seat facing down the ridge. Both men sat there silently until Tom returned with two additional deputies. Joe instructed the new arrivals to take positions where they could keep an eye out on the group. There wasn't a lot that could be done until the Medical Examiner arrived. Tom once again retreated down the ridge to the water's edge and waited for yet another boat to arrive.

Tom was sitting on the flattest rock he could find protruding from the soil of the lake point when he heard the roar of the outboard motor. As he turned, he recognized the Tennessee Valley Authority (TVA) boat quickly approaching. He came to his feet and waved his hand high in the air. Now the morning temperature was starting to climb as the sun cleared the mountain, and the rays were beginning to shine directly onto most of the lake. Only small parts of the water remained shady due to the sunshine being blocked by the tall ridges that surrounded the lake. Soon the entire area would be buzzing with the summer activities of the local population.

The Medical Examiner slid off the bow of the boat just as it slid onto the soft soil adjacent to the rocky point. Once securing his foothold on the shore, the Examiner looked at Tom and asked, "What have we got?"

Tom replied, "Not sure, sir... The victim's up on the ridge."

Neil Bowman was a tall, slender man in his late 30s; he had worked for the Examiner's Office ever since graduating from college. Neil took a quick glance up the hill and asked, "What's somebody doing up there?"

Tom raised his eyebrows and replied, "Don't believe he went up there on his own free will, Neil."

Neil cocked his head a little and asked, "He was carried up there?"

Tom answered, "Appears he was pulled out of the front of his boat next to the shore over there, then he was dragged to the top of the ridge. And then… then… his…"

"Then what, Tom?" asked Neil.

Tom just looked Neil straight in his eyes. "Come on, Neil… Follow me. You got to see this for yourself; maybe you can make some sense of this."

Neil adjusted the straps on his backpack, and the two men began the trek to the top of the ridge. Neil followed exactly in Tom's footsteps as they navigated between the trees. Tom led the Examiner up a much easier way to the top of the ridge, just as he had done for the later arriving deputies. No sense in climbing the more treacherous part of the ridge more than once in a day.

As the two men arrived upon the scene, the entire group of individuals that were already there came to their feet. Only the lone deputy keeping a vigil on the area he had been watching remained motionless as the two men approached the body. Joe sensed it was merely a self-perseveration mode that the deputy was in, rather than guarding the body of the deceased individual. All the men exchanged greetings, and Neil carefully made his way to the body lying on the forest floor. He took note of the drag marks left in the leaves leading to the spot where the victim lay. Next, he glanced to the area where the ridge started descending down to the water.

Joe interrupted the Examiner's thoughts, "It looks like that all the way down to the shoreline; even the lake bank has drag marks."

Neil looked directly at Joe as he continued to give him a complete rundown of everything that had taken place, from the time the fishermen found the woman in the boat right up until he walked up on the scene. As Neil turned his attention back to the body again, Joe remembered the part about the howl and how it terrified the woman. Joe added, "Oh yeah… There was a long howl somewhere on the mountain. The two fishermen said the woman went into a panic mode when she heard it, almost started fighting the guy that was holding her."

Joe immediately noticed the odd facial expression on the deputy that had been diligently guarding the scene as he looked around at the group. Everyone else was either staring at the body or Neil as he continued to examine the victim, and nobody else noticed the strange look on the man's face. Neil carefully examined the body and the area surrounding it; he took countless pictures of everything, paying close attention to the deep gashes on the man's throat. Soon they placed the body into a bag and began the journey down to the shoreline. Each time Joe glanced at the deputy, he was met with the man's eyes looking back at him.

When they finally reached the shoreline, the gentlemen carrying the victim placed the body into one of the TVA boats to be transported to the waiting ambulance at the loading ramp. Neil climbed in, and the boat sped away. As everyone was boarding their respective boats for their return trip to the ramp, Joe turned to the younger deputy and asked, "How about you help us get the victim's boat back?"

The young deputy agreed and climbed into the boat with Phil and Joe. Phil wasn't sure of what was going on, since he or Joe could have driven the victim's boat while the other piloted the TWRA craft. Finally, the situation got the best of Phil, and he asked, "What's the deal here, guys? You and I could have got the boat back, Joe."

Joe looked at the deputy and responded, "I noticed your reaction when I mentioned the howl... and I noticed you looking in my direction quite a lot coming off that ridge."

The young deputy stretched forth his hand. He said, "My name's Roger Dalby... I'd like to talk with you guys privately, Agent Wales."

Joe shook the deputy's hand. "You mean somewhere besides here and now? Ain't gonna get much more private than this."

Roger replied, "How about we exchange personal numbers and meet at a time we are all off the timeclock? I really don't want the other guys to know that I am talking to you. Some of them already think I'm a little paranoid. I've heard that howl too... more than once. I need someone to believe my story."

The men exchanged numbers and agreed to meet a few nights later. The deputy climbed into the victim's boat and followed the TWRA officers back to the loading ramp. Once the boat was loaded onto the trailer, the deputy drove the victim's truck and trailer to the local police holding garage.

CHAPTER 7

The days had turned into weeks. Both Sonny and Billy were beginning to wonder if they were ever going to hear from Rhonda. Ironically, Sonny's phone rang on June the 22nd around 4 p.m. It was Rhonda calling on the very afternoon after the occurrence on South Holston Reservoir. She asked Sonny if it would be possible for all of them to get together and talk in private. Sonny suggested for her to come over to the house that evening. He said he would give Billy a call, and Sarah would serve pie for the group. Rhonda readily agreed to the invitation and hung up the phone. Sonny dialed Billy's number.

At 7:30 that evening, Rhonda pulled her jeep into Sonny and Sarah's driveway. Right away, she noticed that Billy had arrived before her by the presence of his blue Silverado truck parked next to Sarah's vehicle. So, everyone was waiting on her arrival. She thought to herself, *I only wish I had more answers than questions.* As Rhonda walked toward the steps to the wrap-around porch of the chalet-style house, she gently slid her hand along the engine hood of Billy's truck. She realized that he hadn't arrived much earlier by the warm paint and metal of the engine hood.

Three knocks on the door, and Rhonda could hear footsteps coming through the living room of the house. The door opened, and Sarah smiled at Rhonda. Sarah said, "Come on in, Rhonda. Just took the pie out of the oven."

Rhonda could already smell the aroma of the pie. She grinned and replied, "Thanks, the pie smells good. Sure could use a slice of it and a hot cup of coffee."

Sarah closed the door after Rhonda entered the living room, then pointed to the kitchen and said, "Sonny and Billy are waiting at the table. Have a seat, and I'll get that pie. Oh, and four cups of coffee too... Gotta have something to wash down the pie."

Rhonda laughed as she walked across the hardwood floors and made her way to the door opening that led into the kitchen area. As she passed through the opening, she immediately saw the small wooden table that Sonny and Billy were sitting at. When the men noticed Rhonda entering the room, they both began to push their chairs back and rose to their feet. Rhonda held out her hand and said, "Whoa, boys, no need to get all formal about this. Just keep your butts in them seats."

Both Sonny and Billy eased back into the chairs as Rhonda pulled out the only remaining one, placed in its rightful spot under the edge of the table. It was obvious that Sarah had been sitting at the table with the men as they waited on Rhonda to arrive. Sarah placed four light tan cups on the table and the coffee pot on a protective pad right in the center. Next, she brought four plates, two at a time, with a generous helping of the homemade apple pie. In her last return to the table, she brought the half gallon of vanilla ice cream, which she placed next to the coffee pot and dug the scoop into it.

Sarah was already familiar with the way that Sonny and Billy liked their pie. She placed a scoop of the ice cream on each man's pie. When she glanced at Rhonda, she got an affirmative nod from her, so Sarah dug another scoop out and placed it on Rhonda's slice. All three thanked Sarah, and everybody dug into their servings. About the only conversation heard at the table was the compliments directed at Sarah for her ability to make the perfect apple pie.

After the food was consumed, Sarah returned the ice cream to the freezer, the four people re-filled their cups, and the two men leaned back into their chairs. Rhonda was sitting and leaning forward with both forearms resting on the edge of the table. She held the coffee cup with both hands. As she stared into the cup, she said, "I wish I had more answers for you guys... but I don't."

Billy looked at Sonny and then back to Rhonda. "What about the hair that Sarah found? What did your friend make of it?"

Rhonda looked around the table and then focused directly on Sonny. She slightly raised her eyebrows and said, "We're totally off the record here, people... I really like my job, and I don't want to jeopardize it in any way. Are we all in agreement?"

Sonny replied, "Okay... What are we exactly saying here?"

Rhonda took a deep breath and exhaled a long sigh, "Everyone has to promise that our conversation doesn't leave this house."

Billy leaned forward and placed his hands on the table, then he asked, "So, whatever we discuss has to be kept secret between the four of us?"

Rhonda replied, "Yes."

Everyone agreed, and Rhonda began to speak, "I found it very odd that the state did not return the evidence bag that contained the hair. I plainly told you guys that out in the woods that day."

"So, they still haven't returned it yet?" Sonny asked.

Rhonda shook her head and answered, "No... When the report came back that it was of unknown origin and probably a bear's hair, we requested to have it returned so we could analyze it further. Just a couple of days later, the report came back that the hair belonged to a bear, and the case was closed."

Billy raised his hands off the table and rotated them to a thumbs-up position. Next, he stated, "We never got informed on the fact that the case was closed. We figured that it was still under investigation."

Sonny chimed in, "Billy's right… Every time it's been mentioned, our boss seems to believe the state is still investigating whatever took place that night along the trail."

Rhonda reiterated, "I was informed that the culprit was a bear, and the state had already notified the families. Then I was told that the case was closed, and no further investigation is required. This is why this conversation cannot leave this house, okay?"

Sonny nodded yes. "I understand why now… What about the hair Sarah found?"

Rhonda glanced down at the coffee mug and said, "Well… I'm not gonna tell you guys what my friend's name is simply because she wants to remain anonymous. She is pretty perplexed about the hair and what she was able to determine in her analysis of it. Of course, she is kinda in the same boat as we are."

This time, Sarah interrupted, "And what kinda boat is that?"

Rhonda grinned. "She has more questions than answers too. She determined that the hair doesn't belong to any known animal we have inhabiting the park."

Billy spoke next, "But this animal was in the park."

Rhonda responded, "Exactly… and there's no doubt it killed those two individuals."

Sonny tilted his head and tapped the middle finger of his right hand on the table twice. Then he stated, "If the state believed there was a rogue bear roaming the park, we would be exercising every effort possible to locate it."

Rhonda added, "You're absolutely right… I think the state is as confused about the hair as my friend."

Sonny asked, "And just what does she think?"

Rhonda rubbed her forehead and answered, "She says the hair exhibits the characteristics of a wolf."

Billy looked around the table, then back at Rhonda. He said, "We have coyotes and wolves in the park."

Rhonda smiled and said, "Yes, but this hair doesn't match any known wolf in the United States, let alone in the Great Smoky National Park."

Sonny asked, "Then what kind of wolf does it match?"

Rhonda shook her head once again as she spoke to the other three, "There are no known matches."

"So, there's nothing else we can do?" asked Billy.

Rhonda replied, "Not that I know of... We'll just have to wait and see if there are more developments later on."

Sonny heavily sighed and said, "I hope those developments don't include another victim."

Rhonda replied, "Yeah... Me too."

It was just beginning to get dark on Thursday of the following week when Joe and Phil made the turn into Roger Dalby's driveway. After placing the truck in park, Joe set the emergency brake on the vehicle. He turned the key, and the motor went silent. Almost immediately, the floodlight aimed at the wooden steps leading up to the deck came on. Both men exited the truck, when about halfway to the steps a voice welcomed them to the residence. The agents looked up and waived at the figure standing at the top step with one hand firmly gripping the handrail.

Joe was the first to speak, "Nice place you got here, Roger."

Roger replied with a smile, "Thanks. Luckily my wife is a manager at her company. Somebody in this marriage has to be able to afford this. Thankfully she hasn't kicked me out yet."

Just then, a petite woman with shoulder length auburn hair appeared at the side of Roger. She laughed and said, "He better not push his luck, though."

Both Joe and Phil chuckled. Phil was still smiling when he reached the top of the steps. Then Phil pointed at Roger and said, "Sounds like you better walk a straight line, buddy."

Roger extended his hand to the two agents and said, "Believe me… I do. Come on, let's go inside."

Roger's wife, Ellen, led the way into the house and Roger closed the door once he was inside. Right away, Joe and Phil noticed that the house was spotless, and everything was in its rightful place. Even the three magazines sitting on the coffee table right in front of the couch were neatly stacked. There were two lamps resting on doilies on the end tables beside each arm of the couch. Both lamps were on.

Ellen broke the silence, "Can I get you guys something to drink?" Then she added, "We have tea, soft drinks, and coffee."

Phil opted for the tea, and Joe asked for a cup of coffee. Roger asked the guys to take a seat. Joe sat on the burgundy and gray plaid couch at the end facing the magazines. Phil sat in the wooden rocker beside the fireplace. Roger sat in his favorite place, the leather recliner, and within a couple of minutes, Ellen started delivering the drinks.

Joe leaned forward on the couch and asked, "So, what is it that you wanted to share with us, Roger?"

Ellen took a seat on the other end of the couch as Roger began to speak, "Like I told you down at the lake… I've heard those howls also. Ellen has heard them too. They're really strange, guys. We've also noticed some weird things… things we just can't explain."

Joe glanced at Ellen, who was simply staring at her glass of tea, and then focused back on Roger. "What kind of strange things?"

Roger placed his glass on a coaster on the small table located beside his recliner. "Listen, guys… I don't want my name tied to any of this. It's not only *what* we have witnessed but *where* we saw it."

Phil asked, "Where might that be?"

Ellen looked up from her glass and said, "Right off our front porch."

Joe turned and locked in on Ellen's eyes. "You mean along the road... in the woods... or what?"

Both agents turned back to Roger when he began to speak, "At the house across the street from our driveway. Do you guys know who lives there?"

Phil responded, "Have no idea... Can't say I've ever been in this part of the county before."

Roger took a deep breath and exhaled the air, "That is Eva Mae Shelton's house. She and her two sons live there. Her sons are Ronnie and Ricky. Ronnie is 21 and Ricky is 19. As far as we know, they are really good boys. I think they both attend a local college but are still living at home. They are always helping their mom around the house and on the property. Both are really hard workers. They always offered a helping hand to any of the neighbors when needed. They've helped us on several occasions."

Phil asked, "Who exactly is Eva Mae Shelton?"

Ellen answered, "Probably one of the most influential women of the area; loads of money passed down from the family. But neither her nor her sons flaunt the fact that they are rich. If you met them out on the town, you would never know they had money."

Roger took a sip of his drink, placed his glass back on the coaster, and stated, "Listen, guys... I know the laws that apply to spying on your neighbors, but I want to show you a video we captured from our deck. This just happened to be the same night that whatever happened to that guy on the ridge at the lake occurred. Ellen and I were in bed when our two dogs began to growl. They left the bedroom and came into this room like they were stalking something. When I got in here, they were standing firmly in their tracks, staring at the front door. The hair on both dogs was standing straight up, and they both were showing their teeth. As I approached the window to look out, one of the dogs stood next to me on the left side and the other on the right. They followed every movement I made like they were guarding me. I had never seen them act that way before."

Phil interrupted, "What dogs?"

Ellen answered, "Ben and Jerry... You know, like the ice cream. They're German Shepherds. We put them in the bedroom just before you guys got here."

Joe grinned and asked, "For our protection?"

Ellen laughed, "No... Well, maybe. They won't bite, but they just might lick you to death. We usually put them in the bedroom when we have company. Some people might not enjoy having dogs that size trying to sit on their laps and licking them in the face."

Roger began to speak again, "The dogs never wavered from their mode of protection until the lights down at Eva Mae's were turned off. After that, they followed me back into the bedroom and laid back down on their beds. I don't know if they went back to sleep or not. All I know is I laid there with my eyes wide open until daybreak, but that really wasn't that long... Maybe 45 minutes or an hour."

Then Joe asked, "But what you saw and captured on film... It was down at this Eva Mae's house?"

Roger answered, "Yes, sir."

Phil cleared his throat, "I'm sure you had a good reason for aiming a camera at that house. Anyone else seen the footage?"

Roger shook his head. "No, sir... Like I said, some of my buddies at work believe I'm a little paranoid. I like watching those kinds of shows on the ole television–you know, the paranormal shows. Plus, there's more to this situation than just one rich lady and her two sons."

Phil asked, "How so, Roger?"

Roger replied, "Let's watch the film footage and I'll explain."

CHAPTER 8

Roger rose from the recliner and made his way across the room to a shelf above the desk that the computer was sitting on. He removed a small wooden box between two books and opened the lid. He lifted the flash drive out and turned to the agents. Then Roger said, "Everybody, gather around the computer... You'll want to watch this from up close."

Joe, Phil, and Ellen all made their way to the desk. Ellen directed the two men to each side of Roger as he sat down in the black leather swivel chair. Roger placed the thumb drive into the proper slot and loaded the file for viewing. It was obvious that Roger and Ellen had the recording device set up for motion detection. The dark pickup truck was the first object appearing on the video.

The camera was recording by thermal imaging. The exhaust of the truck was glowing reddish yellow. Next, the driver's door opened, and a figure exited the truck. One could follow the image as it walked to the house and up the steps onto the porch. Once the door to the house was opened, the heat signature came back down the steps and walked to the rear of the truck. The next movements of the glowing red figure were what appeared to be the raising of a camper top cover and the lowering of the tailgate.

After the figure took a slow look at the surroundings, it stepped back and made a sweeping motion with one arm. The next two heat signatures that the agents witnessed caught them totally off guard. One at a time, the red images leaped from the back of the truck to the pavement of the driveway. In single file, they rounded the rear of the vehicle and raced to the steps on all fours. The first figure bounded up the steps on all fours, while the second one appeared to come to a bipedal position and walked up the steps on its hind legs. Just as the first figure disappeared through the door, the second creature dropped back on all fours and bolted into the house.

Both agents focused on the heat signature at the rear of the truck. They watched silently as it closed the back of the truck and made its way to the house. Once inside, the light came on and the front door closed. There was nothing else on the film, and the recording ended as the camera timer reached the point of it recognizing no more movement. All four people continued to stare at the computer screen. The two agents tried to determine exactly what they had just witnessed.

Finally, Joe broke the silence and asked, "What were those two things that came out the back of the truck? Dogs?"

Ellen responded, "There are no dogs at Eva Mae's house."

Joe pivoted and faced Ellen. "But they looked like dogs when they jumped out of the bed of the truck."

Roger swiveled his chair to face Joe. "Ever seen a dog climb stairs like a human? Besides, both of them animals were pretty big, sir."

Phil was still staring at the blank computer screen when he asked, "Can we watch that footage again?"

The four people watched the video three more times, and each time it only created more questions than answers. When the video ended for the third time, Joe placed his hand on Roger's shoulder and said, "Let's start from the beginning... Just when did you get suspicions of something strange going on?"

Roger rose from the computer chair and walked back to the recliner. The other three returned to the seats they occupied before viewing the video. Once seated, all eyes focused on Roger as he began to explain, "Probably about five months ago... Ellen and I came back late one night. We opened the door to let the dogs out to use the bathroom. The night air was pretty brisk; it was a crystal-clear night. The moon was full, and you could see a million stars. As we waited on the deck for the dogs to finish, somewhere near the top of the mountain there was a long, drawn-out howl. Just a few seconds later, there was a second howl. It sounded really close to the first one but just a little ways down the mountain. Both of the dogs immediately froze in their tracks. Then they started to growl and show their teeth. That was really odd for Ben and Jerry; they have never been aggressive in any manner. So, I told them to come on, and they ran back up the steps to us. We went inside... but they kinda acted odd the rest of the night."

Joe interrupted, "What do you mean?"

Ellen answered, "It was like they were guarding us; they wouldn't leave our side."

Then Roger spoke, "After an hour or so, I heard a door shut... I got out of bed, walked to the front room, and looked out the window. I saw Eva Mae's light come on in the front room of the house. Ben followed me and was standing right beside me."

"Where was Jerry?" Phil asked.

Roger responded, "When Ben and I walked back into the bedroom, Jerry was sitting on the floor next to Ellen. I crawled back into bed, and in a few minutes both dogs laid down on their beds. That was the first time they had relaxed since we heard the howls out on the porch."

"Anything else odd?" asked Phil.

Roger explained, "From the night we heard the howls up on the mountain, we've noticed that ever so often, the dogs act uneasy... It always seems to be isolated to just a single night, though. Then, the next day, they begin to act normal again. It's really strange. The dogs stick very close to us like they are protecting us from someone or something."

Joe asked, "Is that the only video you have?"

Roger shook his head and answered, "Yes, and you are the only people we have shown it to. We started doing our own investigation after the dogs began to act irrational, being the paranormal freak that I am. Since I am a deputy for the county, I have a few avenues for searching that the normal individual probably doesn't have access to, so Ellen and I started searching for oddities."

"And I'm assuming that some oddities clearly came into view?" Joe asked.

Ellen smiled and said, "Yeah... We found a few."

"Like what?" Phil asked.

Roger cleared his throat and replied, "We found several reports where farm animals had been killed and mutilated. In the reports, almost all of them had been contributed to some kind of wild animal. You know—a bear, mountain lion, coyote—something along that line."

Phil chimed in next, "Yeah, a lot of that kind of stuff doesn't warrant much time for investigation."

Roger added, "Yeah... Most of the time, the farmer gets compensated and that's that."

Then Joe asked, "How long ago did these reports take place?"

Roger tilted his head slightly and said, "That's the strange part. Up until about a year and a half ago, the reports were very sporadic. Then all of a sudden, there was a report coming in every month. I've been summoned to a couple of the local ones myself."

"So, there have been more in other places?" asked Phil.

Roger nodded and said, "Yes... The reports come from a variety of areas; never a report from the same county two months in a row. Then, last fall during deer season, there was a report in Virginia of two hunters being killed up on the mountain above Damascus. I don't know if you guys ever heard of the town, but it's famous in these parts for hikers of the Appalachian Trail and bicycle enthusiasts on the Virginia Creeper Trail. Heck, even a president came down and rode the trail from Whitetop Mountain down to Damascus."

Phil interrupted, "Oh yeah, I've read some info on the trail. Used to be an old railroad, right?"

Roger continued, "Yes. Nice, scenic ride. Take a shuttle to the top of the mountain and enjoy the scenery on the easy cruise down the mountain. But as I was saying, apparently these two guys were camping for the entire first week of the deer hunting season. I think it was Tuesday or Wednesday of that week that their wives fixed some supper and went to hang out with the guys at the campsite. There was no cellphone service in the area, so the women expected nothing outside the norm since they hadn't called before going to visit. Just take the boys some grub and sit by the campfire for a while."

Joe asked, "And what happened when they got there?"

Roger answered, "When the women first pulled up to the campsite, everything was dark... There were no lanterns illuminating the tent, and the campfire was completely out. The two women exited their SUV, turned on flashlights, and started toward the tent. Right away, they noticed one of the tent poles was broken and small items were scattered about. But there was nothing that prepared them for what they found lying in the leaves beside the tent."

"One of the men?" Joe asked.

Roger sighed and replied, "Yes... Of course, the women were terrified, so they ran back to the vehicle and locked the doors. They drove down the mountain until they got a cell signal and called the authorities. Soon the area was crawling with law enforcement and emergency personnel. It took about 30 minutes, but they found the second hunter about 200 yards from the campsite."

Phil asked, "Had he been dragged there?"

Roger shrugged his shoulders and said, "The next day, the officers continued to investigate the area, but it didn't appear he had been dragged at all. Apparently, he was running through the woods in the dark... no flashlight or anything. He did have a pistol, which by the way, had been fired several times. There was still one bullet left in the chamber, but the clip was empty. It appeared that he had fired the gun six times, but obviously to no avail, and he never got to fire that last shell."

Joe placed his hands in the pockets of his khaki pants and walked to the fireplace. Then he turned back to Roger and said, "I'm assuming they tested the gun to make sure he had indeed fired the weapon."

Roger replied, "Yes, sir. They actually found a couple of the shell casings between the tent and where he lay."

Then Joe asked, "And you think this is relevant to the guy at the lake?"

Roger nodded and said, "The internal organs of the two hunters were also missing, but the investigation yielded no definitive answers, and the final conclusion was that it was the work of one or more wild animals."

Phil rose to his feet. "Holy mackerel," he interjected. "That's three people in less than a year that's been discovered in that condition."

Roger looked at Phil, "Not exactly... You can add two more to that list."

Joe lifted his head to look at Roger as Phil slowly sank back into his seat. Then Joe asked, "What two?"

Roger explained, "Around a month and a half ago, there was an incident down in the Great Smoky Mountains, just right above Gatlinburg. Two hikers were killed out in the woods beside the Sugarland Mountain Trail. The female was found at the campsite while the male victim was located approximately a hundred yards away. The internal organs were missing on both of the hikers. It also appeared that the male individual was running for his life in the darkness of the forest."

Phil placed one hand over the other and asked, "He took off running without her? He just left her?"

Roger hesitated for just a second and then answered, "Nobody knows for sure what exactly transpired in the woods that night... But whatever it was, it must have terrified the man. Look at the deer hunter's situation. What would provoke a seasoned outdoorsman to run from a campsite with just a pistol and no flashlight? For crying out loud, there were two high powered rifles lying in the tent. Why didn't he use one of them?"

Joe cleared his throat and asked, "So now, we are talking about five people in less than a year that have sustained similar injuries?"

"Yes," Ellen responded.

Phil added, "But in three totally different locations."

Roger replied, "Yes, three different areas. But all five have matching injuries. I told you this really got strange, guys."

Joe glanced at the computer, and silence filled the room. Finally, he turned to face the others and asked, "Roger, did you and Ellen happen to find in your search who investigated the Smoky Mountain incident?"

Roger answered, "Yes. Two day hikers found the male victim beside the trail. The male hiker led the investigative and recovery team to the body, but a couple of park rangers called it in. They were the first to confer with the hiker and his wife. One of the rangers is Sonny Rutherford, and the second one is Billy Rogers. But if you are going to try and contact them, you might want to be a little discreet about it."

"And why's that?" asked Joe.

This time, Ellen answered, "Well... The state has already closed the case."

Phil asked, "Boy, that's quick. Wonder why?"

Roger responded, "Don't know... That's another oddity that we found."

Joe walked over to the window and stared down at the house across from the couple's driveway, then turned to face the group. Slowly he slid his teeth across his lower lip and asked, "Wonder if we can get permission to put some kind of surveillance on that house?"

"That might be kinda tough," Roger replied, then explained further, "Eva Mae's sister is married to one of the prominent judges of the county."

Phil placed both hands onto his knees. "Oh, this just gets better and better, Joe." He turned to look at Roger and said, "Now I know why you didn't want your name mentioned... I'm not sure if I want to be involved either."

Joe chuckled, “I think we are in too deep now to turn back; it’s either sink or swim, ole boy.”

Phil only mustered a small smirk when he said, “I’m not gonna sink… You know I always wear a life jacket.”

The other three laughed, then Joe said, “Give me the judge’s name and I will set up a meeting with him. Somehow, I’ll try to convince him of some kind of surveillance on his sister-in-law. Make me a copy of that flash drive. I may just have to use it as a tool. And if you don’t care, write down those park rangers’ names. We’ll try to set a meeting with them in private. Phil, maybe the four of us can compare notes.”

Ellen walked over to the computer and sat down; she quickly made a copy of the flash drive and placed the original back into the wooden box. Next, she took a pad from the desk drawer and wrote down the rangers’ names. Joe thanked her as he placed the objects in his shirt pocket. He buttoned the pocket for the safe keeping of the flash drive and the names on the paper.

Then Joe turned to Roger to say, “I’ll not mention you or Ellen at any time. Let me see what we can find out and I’ll get back to you.”

Ellen said, “We appreciate it… but keep us in the loop if you don’t care.”

Joe responded, “I promise. Thanks for the coffee, and one of us will give you guys a call.”

The two men said their goodbyes and made their way back to the truck. As they pulled out of the driveway, neither of them could prevent themselves from taking a quick glance at Eva Mae’s house.

CHAPTER 9

The warm summer nights had become a common occurrence. It was now July the 21st, and this night was no different. There had been no new developments for the rangers and Rhonda in the Great Smoky Mountain National Park.

Joe and Phil had been waiting for a couple of weeks to meet with the judge. Apparently, his schedule was pretty busy, and the two men didn't want to push the issue. Consulting with the man about his sister-in-law was going to be challenging enough.

Not far from the oldest town in Tennessee, Jonesborough, lies a river basin with beautiful farmland where strawberries and other various produce are grown. The Nolichucky River flows through the area and the numerous fields that border it. The fields eventually give way to the mountain range that guards the area by towering over the majestic view.

Shawn and Abby owned a small farm on the opposite side of the road from the river; the property ran right up to the base of the mountain at the National Forest property boundary. Just before the tree line at the upper end of the field was a horse barn that was surrounded by a wooden fence. The grass was bright green and looked like a lush carpet surrounding the barn. The horses had already been placed in their stalls for the night. Dinner had been eaten a couple of hours ago, and now it was time to relax and soak up the warm night air.

The couple was sitting on the front porch. Abby was thumbing through social media on her phone. This was a peaceful night for the two of them; no grandkids at the house for the weekend. Just Shawn, Abby, and the two family dogs. One of the dogs, a chocolate lab, was lying between the rocking chairs the couple occupied. The second dog, an Australian shepherd, was sound asleep at the top of the steps.

Suddenly, the Australian shepherd raised its head and stared into the darkness above the house. It was followed by the lab, which came to a sitting position and turned toward the barn. Abby didn't recognize the movements of the dogs but took notice when Shawn leaned forward in the rocker he was sitting in. She then whispered, "What's wrong?"

Shawn didn't respond at first, but when she started to speak again, he held out his hand to stop her. After a couple of seconds, Shawn finally responded, "There's something at the barn. Got the horses all stirred up."

Abby leaned forward and said, "We better go check on them."

Shawn was still staring at the barn when he replied, "Probably another bear... Let's put the dogs inside and I'll go check it out."

Both Shawn and Abby eased out of the rocking chairs and convinced the dogs to come inside. Shawn grabbed his pistol, a flashlight, and started out the door. Abby was right on his heels. When they walked onto the front porch, Shawn instructed Abby to stay there with the dogs. He assured her that he would be alright. As he got to the steps, Shawn switched on the flashlight, turned to Abby with a smirk on his face, and said, "If I don't come back... take good care of the dogs."

Abby frowned and replied, "Maybe we should all go."

Then Shawn smiled and responded, "The last thing we need is to have the dogs take off chasing a bear, or even worse, get into a fight with one. If you hear me shoot, then I may need some help. Probably everybody in the neighborhood will come running after I wake them up."

Abby watched as Shawn started up the dirt road that led to the barn, and suddenly it dawned on her that she didn't have a weapon if Shawn did indeed run into trouble. Abby quickly retreated back into the house to get her firearm. On her way out of the bedroom, she picked up the spotlight lying on the desk beside the door. Swiftly she navigated around the couch and passed through the front door onto the porch. Abby noticed from the flashlight beams that Shawn was near the barn, and now the rays of light seemed to be searching all around the structure. The one thing that didn't register in Abby's mind was the fact that the screen door had failed to latch completely as it closed.

Shawn could hear the horses stirring in their respective stalls. Every now and then, one of the horses would kick the hemlock boards that made up the walls of the stalls. He paused about 30 yards from the two sliding doors at the entrance to the barn. Shawn carefully shined the light around his surroundings in search of whatever was causing the horses' excitement. With one hand on the pistol and the other manipulating the flashlight, he suddenly realized something: the darkness that surrounded him and the barn was eerily quiet. It was dead silent, no little creatures scurrying around. There weren't even any sounds from the multitude of crickets that inhabited the ankle-deep grass of the barn lot.

Back on the porch of the house, Abby intently watched the activity up at the barn, even though all she could see was the beam of the flashlight as it scanned the darkness. One of the dogs let out a small whine, wanting to join Abby on the porch. She was quick to snap her fingers to silence the dog. It hadn't occurred to her just how quiet the moment had become; she thought once of walking up the hill to join Shawn, but for some reason she remained on the porch, leaning against the post where the steps met the floor of the deck.

All of a sudden, Shawn heard movement around the left side of the barn. It almost sounded like something hard sliding against the outside hemlock planks. He methodically moved his feet through the grass to a position where he could shine the light in that direction, and just as the light protruded through the darkness Shawn caught a glimpse of a figure as it moved around the back corner.

Shawn didn't believe his eyes at first. He wasn't sure of what to make of the thing he had just seen. His brain quickly diagnosed that the object was indeed black like a bear, but it appeared to be moving in an upright position. It made no sense in Shawn's mind. The next second, there were several loud thuds as the horses jostled and kicked the stall walls. Shawn was still fixated on the left side of the barn when the attack came from behind him. There had been no time to see the culprit—only a split second of sound as the creature left the ground and leaped onto Shawn's back.

The impact caused Shawn to careen forward, and in his effort to grip the flashlight and gun, he inadvertently pulled the trigger. The expulsion of the bullet pierced the warm night air and echoed through the valley down below. Shawn planted face first into the dew-soaked grass at almost the same spot the bullet impacted the ground. Right away, he could feel the burning sensation on his back where the creature's claws had penetrated his skin as it pounced on him. In a moment of panic, his entire body kicked into survival mode. Shawn rolled onto his burning back and fired another round into the direction the attacker had come from. But there was nothing there. When Shawn aimed the flashlight, it only lit up an empty void.

As soon as the first shot rang out, Abby sprang into motion. Her feet only touched two of the steps climbing to the porch. She stumbled as her right foot came into contact with the concrete sidewalk, but after a couple of off-balance maneuvers, Abby was upright and sprinting toward the barn.

Shawn was trying to get to his feet when the next attack came from the left side of the barn. Something grabbed him just as the flashlight found one of the creatures standing about 20 feet away next to the barn lot gate. The next thing that Shawn realized was that his feet were no longer touching the ground, and his body was being hurled through the air. The impact with the ground nearly knocked the wind out of him, but now his body was running on fear and adrenalin. Shawn immediately came to his feet, gasping for air. As the flashlight illuminated the black silhouette, he squeezed the trigger, but the creature had already begun its evasive maneuver. The bullet raced through the darkness until it collided with a tree in the surrounding woods.

When Abby passed through the gate, she screamed Shawn's name. Her spotlight caught the creature that Shawn had last fired the gun at. It was in mid-air as it leaped at him, much too close for Abby to take a chance by firing a shot. Once again Shawn was slammed to the ground and was fighting for his life. As she watched in horror, Abby heard a snarling growl to her right. As she pivoted in that direction, there was a large black figure running toward her. Abby only had a split second to pull the trigger, but her entire body froze.

Just before the creature collided with Abby, she screamed at the top of her lungs. The high-pitched tone echoed throughout the mountain and raced back down to the couple's house. The Australian shepherd pushed its nose against the door, and it swung open. Both dogs bounded down the steps and raced toward the barn. Their paws slapped the dirt of the road as they ran at full speed up the hill. The dogs were in full-on protection mode, and their only mission was to defend their owners.

The Australian shepherd was the first to pass through the open gate. The dark figure hovering over Abby came into view. At a distance of about five feet, all four paws of the Australian shepherd left the ground. Next, it opened its jaws. With a loud thud, the dog impacted the creature, sinking its teeth into the hairy side of the black figure. The creature exhaled a shrill scream as the dog's teeth pierced its skin, and it was jolted off Abby and landed in the wet grass.

The chocolate lab never broke stride as he passed Abby. The dog leaped into the air and clamped down on the second creature's arm as it attempted to deliver the fatal strike to Shawn's chest. The momentum of the impact rolled the creature off of Shawn and onto its back. The next strike from the dog was clearly aimed at the creature's throat but slightly missed as the attacker tried to come up on all fours. The lab's teeth sliced the skin on the creature's head just above the right ear, and the creature growled as it swung one of its arms in a sweeping motion. The lab was already in kill mode and somehow had anticipated the creature's next move. The sweeping arm with extended claws merely moved through the night air, making contact with nothing.

The next sound in the darkness was the angry squall exhaled by the creature that attacked Abby as the Australian shepherd sunk its teeth into its leg, but before it could deliver a counterattack, the dog had already positioned itself for the lunge at the creature's neck. Just at that moment, Abby regained her composure and came to her knees. She could hear all the snarling and growling as the two animals close to her continued to fight. Just as the Australian shepherd started to make its move, Abby fired the pistol. The bullet passed within inches of the creature and raced through the darkness toward the trees of the forest. The dog merely collided with the dark figure as it came to all fours and began to run to the safety of the mountain.

The lab was contemplating the angle of its next move when the second creature leaped up and began to hastily follow the first one. Abby stumbled over to Shawn, who was holding his chest with two blood-covered hands. Shawn said, "Call somebody and get us some help."

Abby found her phone in the pocket of her shorts just as she heard the voice coming from the road leading to the barn. She turned and screamed, "Up here! Hurry!"

Abby aimed the spotlight toward the tree line above the barn and saw the two pair of red eyes staring in their direction. The dogs had taken a defensive position between the couple and the red, beady eyes. Abby couldn't help but think of the creatures' retreat; one was on all fours and the other was running on two legs. That is, until about halfway through the field. Then it dropped down on all fours as it scurried to the woods.

This time when the voice called out her name, Abby recognized it as belonging to Scott, a middle-aged neighbor of theirs. Abby motioned with the spotlight and yelled, "Over here, Scott! Call 911."

Abby turned back to the tree line and scanned with the spotlight; there were no red eyes shining in the trees. She swept the forest a couple of times with the light, but there was no sign of the creatures that attacked them. The dogs had both sat on the grass but were still facing the forest above. Their demeanor had seemed to calm somewhat.

As Scott approached the couple, he could see the severity of Shawn's injuries and immediately dialed 911. He paced along the path from the gate to the barn, delivering every detail that the dispatcher requested. Abby had knelt onto her knees beside Shawn and was offering all the support that she could muster. She hadn't noticed the two blood-soaked spots at the top of each shoulder of her white T-shirt.

Finally, as Scott finished the call and returned to the couple, he removed his shirt and placed it on Sean's chest. Next, he applied just enough pressure to help with the bleeding. It was only about five minutes until the sound of sirens could be heard coming through the valley. In no time, the deputies and the EMTs were on the scene. After Shawn and Abby were loaded into the ambulance, it sped away to the medical center. Before the doors of the vehicle closed, Scott assured the couple that he would look after the horses and take the dogs to his house. It would be tomorrow before the detectives could question the couple.

Hopefully they could shed some light on what occurred at the barn.

CHAPTER 10

Joseph Wales and Phillip Weaver, the two TWRA agents, pulled their vehicle into the parking at the rear of the Sullivan County Courthouse. As Joe placed the truck into park and set the emergency brake, Phil stared out the passenger side window. The afternoon sun was slowly starting to hide behind the thunderhead clouds forming in the sky. The two men sat silently in the truck for about 20 seconds, then Joe asked, "Ready to go inside?"

Phil turned to Joe, raised his eyebrows slightly, and answered, "I reckon so... I can't wait to see how this little meeting turns out. I just hope we both have jobs tomorrow."

Joe smiled and replied, "Remember... we got a video to bargain with."

Phil shook his head, and both of the agents exited the vehicle. They walked to the entrance of the courthouse without uttering a word. Once inside, they were met by two deputies whose assignment was to clear all individuals who entered the building. Joe informed the deputies that he and Phil had an appointment with Judge William Jones. The deputies checked their credentials and then radioed for someone to come and escort the agents to Judge Jones' chambers.

Not a minute later, a small-statured, middle-aged blonde dressed in a blue skirt and a white blouse introduced herself to the two men. Next, she instructed them to follow her and began to lead the men down the hallway. Phil stared at the back of the woman's head as they walked down the corridor and concluded that she was just about due for her next hair coloring appointment, then he questioned in his own mind why he was even concerned about the lady's hair at all.

As the woman knocked on the door, she simultaneously twisted the knob, and the judge came to his feet as the agents entered the room. The judge stretched forth his hand and stated, "William Jones. Gentlemen, how can I help you?"

Joe and Phil shook the man's hand as they introduced themselves, then both men took a seat in the wooden chairs with the burgundy cushions across from the judge. Joe cleared his throat and began to speak, "We have something we would like to discuss with you... kinda off the record, Mr. Jones. This is really difficult to present to you, but we were the first two agents on the scene out at the lake. You know... the one with the victim on the ridge and his wife floating alone in the boat."

Judge Jones responded, "Yes, that really is a strange one. Haven't heard a lot about the details, though."

Joe rubbed his eyes and lifted his head; he looked the judge directly in the eyes. For just a split second, he almost decided to try and retreat out of the situation. But then he continued to go on with the story. Joe again addressed the judge, "The gentleman on the ridge... When we found him, his internal organs were missing. It appeared that he was grabbed and pulled out of the front of the boat, then according to what we could tell, he was dragged up to the top of the ridge. Mr. Jones, it would be pretty difficult for one to even walk up that incline, let alone drag another human being up it."

Judge Jones asked with a puzzled expression, "Good gosh, boys, what could possibly do that? I mean... you're thinking this was done by some kind of animal, right?"

Phil merely stared at the two men as they took turns speaking. After a small pause, Joe added, "Yes, sir... but this is not the only incident that has occurred with the same type of injuries."

The judge slightly tilted his head and asked, "There have been others?"

Joe answered, "I'm afraid so... There were two deer hunters last season on the mountain above Damascus, Virginia. Then, back in May of this year down in the Great Smoky National Park, a male and a female hiker were killed. All four of these victims had their internal organs missing at the time of the discovery of their bodies."

Judge Jones thought for a second and replied, "That's a pretty large distance between attack sites... but I'm not sure why you guys wanted to meet with me."

Joe knew it was time, so he addressed Judge Jones, "I've got a video that I would like for you to watch. We would really appreciate it."

The judge agreed, and Joe removed the flash drive from his shirt pocket. Mr. Jones plugged the drive into his laptop and within seconds began to view the footage. Both of the agents remained seated on the opposite side of the desk, each intently watching the facial reactions of the judge. It wasn't until the figure, which everyone assumed to be Eva Mae, started up the steps of the house that the judge gasped and looked up. Then he whispered, "Is this Eva Mae Shelton's house?"

Joe answered, "Yes, sir."

"You guys do know that she is my wife's sister?" asked the judge.

Joe responded again, "Yes, sir."

Judge Jones carefully viewed the footage two more times and then removed the flash drive from the computer. He handed it back to Joe, who returned it to his shirt pocket. After buttoning the pocket, Joe started to speak, "Judge..."

Judge Jones lifted his hand to stop Joe. Phil could sense a large lump forming in his throat. Both of the agents were contemplating whether or not to apologize. Then Judge Jones looked at the men and said, "Can you guys come to the house? I believe we need to speak to my wife."

For the first time since introducing himself, Phil spoke, "Are we sure about that, Mr. Jones?"

The judge nodded and answered, "She has an interesting story that just might explain some things to you, especially after she watches this footage."

Both of the agents agreed, and Judge Jones gave them the address. He instructed them to be there around 6:30 and promised that he would not inform his wife that they were coming. As a matter of fact, his wife was busy attending a social event and it may even be close to seven when she arrived, he told the agents. If all went according to plan, the three of them would be at the house when Claire got there.

It was 6:25 when Joe turned the steering wheel and guided the truck into the driveway of William and Claire's house. The home was an older-style brick house with large white columns; the porch not only covered the front of the house but extended down both sides to the back of the house. There were wrought iron railings spanning between the columns, as well as down the steps to the sidewalk. The grass appeared to have been cut recently, and the shrubs were trimmed to perfection.

The front door swung open, and William grinned as he motioned for the agents to come inside. The men once again exchanged greetings as they entered the spacious living room.

Judge Jones offered the men a drink as he removed a glass from the cabinet situated against the far wall. Both of the men declined the offer but graciously thanked the judge. Next, William placed three ice cubes in the glass and removed the cork from what appeared to be an expensive bourbon bottle to the agents. Slowly, he poured the whiskey until the ice cubes were completely covered. After swishing the contents for a couple of seconds, the judge turned to the men, grinned, and said, "You might just change your mind after you hear the wife's story."

Just as Joe was going to inquire about the story, the men heard a car door shut, and William added, "And that should be her now."

When the front door opened, both Joe and Phil turned to face the judge's wife. Claire didn't notice any of the men until she turned from closing the door. She was dressed in off-white pants, accompanied by matching brown shoes and a shirt. Her hair was shoulder-length, auburn-colored, and not a single hair was out of place. Just as Claire's eyes focused on the three gentlemen standing in the living room, William said, "Gentlemen, this is my wife, Claire." Then he pointed at the agents and continued, "Claire, this is Joseph Wales and Phillip Weaver."

The judge laughed as he looked back to the agents and said, "Not too bad for meeting you guys just a little while ago. I'm pretty good with names."

Both Joe and Phil grinned. Then Phil said, "That is pretty impressive, Mr. Jones. Remind me not to break any laws around you."

Next to speak was Claire. "William," she said, "you didn't tell me we were having company. I could have skipped the social and made us all something to eat."

William smiled and said, "Kinda a spur of the moment thing. How did the social go?"

Claire answered, "Same ole thing. One might think some of these women were from royal families with the way they act at these events." Then she turned to the agents and added, "And if you guys ever repeat that, I'll put the royal families hot onto your tails."

Both Joe and Phil chuckled, and Joe said, "No, ma'am... Our lips are sealed."

Claire smiled and looked at the men's shirts. She tilted her head and asked, "What brings TWRA agents to the house?" Then she said to William, "I know they're not here for you doing something illegal while fishing... I can hardly get you to even go to the lake anymore."

William laughed and replied, "Don't be giving my fishing secrets away... We'll have to get us a lawyer."

Claire turned back to the agents and asked, "Did William offer you guys a drink?"

Both men nodded and replied, "Yes, ma'am."

Then Claire held out her hand and said, "Okay... We got to stop with that 'ma'am' stuff."

This time, all three of the men laughed and Claire offered the agents a glass of water or sweet tea. Phil opted for the tea, and as Claire exited the room to prepare the drink, Judge William opened the laptop sitting on the early-1900's rolltop desk. He turned to Joe and asked him for the flash drive. After Joe retrieved it from his shirt pocket, William slid it into the port on the side of the laptop. The judge opened the file just as Claire came back into the room. After she handed the glass to Phil, both men took a seat on the couch. Phil removed a coaster from the set of four sitting on the coffee table and placed the glass onto the coaster.

Judge William swiveled around in the chair and leaned back, and then he sipped a little bourbon from the glass. After a couple of seconds, after the burn of the whiskey subsided, William spoke to his wife, "Claire... These gentlemen let me view a video this afternoon, and I told them that I wanted you to watch it also. Now, these two agents, the person that recorded it, and me are the only people who have viewed this video."

Both Joe and Phil knew that there was one more person in that mix, but there was no need to mention Roger's wife, Ellen, since they both wanted to remain anonymous.

Claire asked as she approached William, "What is in the footage?"

William responded with an unsure look on his face, "I just want to see what you make of it."

He swiveled the chair back to face the computer, and Claire placed her hand on his shoulder. She then said, "Well... let's have a look."

Both agents stared at the backs of the judge and his wife as they watched the video. Claire asked William to play it again as she leaned over and placed both hands on the wooden desk. She never flinched as she viewed the footage for the second time. With her eyes still glued to the screen, she broke the silence as the video ended, "They've broken the seal, William."

William said, "Claire..."

Then Claire abruptly pushed her body into an upright position and turned to glance at the agents. When Claire turned back to face her husband, she said it again: "They've broken the seal, William."

Joe then asked, "What seal?"

Claire took a couple steps away from the desk; her back was to all three men. She crossed her arms and tilted her head toward the ceiling. "The seal of the bottle," she said.

William began to speak, "Claire, could it really be possible for..."

Claire turned to face William. Phil picked up his tea, and the rim of the glass just touched his lips when Claire interrupted William again. With a raised voice, she said, "You saw those two things that got out the back of the truck, and that is Eva Mae's house, William."

The sweet tea just made contact with Phil's lips when he stopped tilting the glass. He could sense the urgency in Claire's voice. William asked if Claire would tell the men about the bottles, so Phil slowly moved the glass back to an upright position and easily placed it back onto the coaster. Claire turned to look at the agents, and after a short silence, she informed them that she would be right back. As Claire exited the room, William walked back to the bourbon bottle and replenished his glass with ice and whiskey. Joe and Phil simply sat in silence waiting for Claire's return.

When she walked back into the room, she placed an old glass flask bottle onto the coffee table. The cork of the bottle was covered in dull white wax that had been rudimentarily dripped onto it and the glass. It was difficult to determine if this was the original color of the glass or if it had lost its luster over time as the wax had. The liquid of the bottle seemed to still be intact, and none had escaped the confines of the bottle.

Claire slid a chair to the opposite side of the coffee table facing the agents, and William took a seat in a large leather recliner to their right. Claire began to speak, "Guys... I would appreciate it if you would listen closely and really think about this tale before you write me off as crazy, okay?"

Both men stared at Claire. William took another sip of his whiskey.

Then Claire continued, "My family's descendants came from a land very far away, and this all started a long time ago. As the story goes, our ancestors lived in Transylvania during the 1600s and 1700s. Over time, we spread out and eventually ended up in the United States around 1900. There are only two of us, Eva Mae and I, plus our children who are left out of the original bloodline. This story has been handed down through many generations, and I'm sure that some details have been lost... Maybe some have been added. But the video we all watched definitely plays the same footage over and over. It's hard to deny that those things that exited the back of the truck are a little strange, to say the least. This story may be a little beyond what we would call normal. All I ask is that you let it sink in for a few minutes before you decide whether you believe it or not."

CHAPTER 11

William sat silently, sipping the whiskey from the glass. The two TWRA agents focused on Claire as she took a deep breath and exhaled the air. For a few seconds, the only sound that was heard was the ticking of the giant Victorian-style clock hanging on the living room wall next to the cabinet bar.

Then Claire began to speak, "In the late 1600s, my great, great grandmother lived in a small village in Transylvania. Several of the family members lived either in the village or the surrounding area. Her oldest sister worked for a man, a Baron, who resided in an old castle on a mountain that overlooked the village. Kinda sound familiar, gentlemen? Almost like the beginning of the old scary movies we watched when we were younger. But this is the story that has been handed down through generations."

Joe glanced at Judge William. He was still sitting motionless in the recliner—all except for his right thumb, which was gently stroking the glass containing the whiskey while the remaining fingers and his palms supported the object.

Claire continued, "The sister never divulged her full duties at the castle, only cleaning and cooking for the old man. That was the story she conveyed. The family of that time had other suspicions, though. The sister never married, and the story goes that as time went on, she became somewhat standoffish to not only the villagers but also to the family. There was also talk of just what the old man did at the castle, and periodically the rumors would run rampant throughout the village."

Joe asked, "What kind of rumors, Mrs. Jones?"

Claire smiled. "Well... just like in the movies, Mr. Wales, the old Baron was a scientist. The people of the village would talk amongst themselves—you know how people do. However, this time, they may have been correct. The sister never would answer any questions directly; she claimed that she merely cleaned and prepared meals for the old man. She inadvertently let it slip about the laboratory beneath the castle one day. Then she added that she very seldom saw the old man due to him spending most of his time there performing his work. When asked about the work done in the laboratory, she only replied that the Baron worked on what we would classify as medicines today. The sister claimed that she never had cleaned the laboratory and really knew nothing about it. The villagers stirred even more amongst themselves with this little tidbit of information; the rumors grew larger and larger. Naturally over time, the people of the village and surrounding area became more uneasy with the Baron and the old castle."

Phil took a sip of tea and then placed the glass gently back onto the coaster, then he looked at Claire and asked, "So, we don't know for sure exactly what the old man was doing?"

Claire responded, "No. Some of the family believes that the sister was well aware of what was happening in that laboratory, but she took most of her secrets to her grave. The only thing she passed along was this bottle, and the one that Eva Mae possesses."

"And what is the significance of the bottles?" asked Joe.

Claire glanced at William and then looked back to the agents, "Well, once again, just like in the movies... the villagers became restless, and in the middle of the night they gathered to storm the castle. They traversed up the mountain with torches and crude weapons in hand. The sister was there late that night when the villagers arrived. The crowd began to pound at the door and demanded to be let inside, but the old man wouldn't beckon to their call. Soon things got out of hand, and the village people set the castle on fire. The sister and the Baron tried to stop the spread of the fire, but it was no use; in just a small amount of time, the entire top portion of the castle was ablaze. The Baron and the sister were forced to retreat into the bottom of the castle—the laboratory room of the structure.

"Soon the floor above them began to cave in on the two of them. The Baron then pushed a large, shelf-like rack away from one of the walls. The rack was hiding a door with a slide latch holding it securely closed. The old man slid the latch and swung open the door. Next, he maneuvered through the fallen debris to a small wooden table, where he retrieved the two bottles. He handed the bottles to the sister and instructed her to make her escape; she turned to face the darkened area beyond the door. The Baron said to follow the tunnel to the spot it ended on the side of the mountain, and not to be afraid. Next, he handed the woman a torch and told her to extinguish it at the opening before emerging from the tunnel. Just before closing the door, the old man instructed her to never let the bottles leave the family and to guard them forever. The seals were never to be broken."

Then Joe asked, "So, I'm assuming the sister followed the old man's instructions?"

Claire replied, "According to the story handed down, she had no choice. The Baron shut the door to the secret passageway, and she heard him slide the latch. After reaching the end of the tunnel, the sister extinguished the torch and made her way to the village. She followed the mountainside so as not to be seen by the mob of villagers. Once the mob returned to the village, a crowd had gathered in the streets to watch the old burning castle. The sister had interwoven herself into the group of onlookers, and not a single person knew that the woman was actually at the castle during the fire."

Phil leaned back onto the couch and asked, "Afterwards... nobody ever questioned the sister about the activities at the castle? And what role do these bottles play, exactly?"

Claire sighed. William looked at the agents and then at Claire. "Explain the bottles, honey," he said.

Claire began, "The woman supposedly never gave any insight to the activities of the castle. The story tells of how, periodically, livestock would be slaughtered in the area but only partially consumed. Seemed that whatever killed the animals had a taste for just the internal organs... mainly the heart. We think that this is what had the villagers in such an uproar about the Baron and the castle, plus the lonely howls the villagers heard coming from the mountains. Finally, on her deathbed, the sister conveyed the part of the story about the bottles. She told my great, great grandmother to never let the bottles leave the family, and to never break the seals, guarding what was inside the bottles."

Joe adjusted his position on the couch and asked, "And just what is inside the bottles, Claire?"

Claire shook her head and said, "Evil, Mr. Wales."

Joe asked, "What kind of evil?"

"The kind of evil you saw getting out the back of that truck," Claire said.

Joe was desperately trying to get a solid answer. He looked Claire directly in the eyes and said, "What exactly did I see getting out the back of the truck?"

Phil had picked up the glass for another sip of the sweet tea, but the glass never made it to his lips as Claire answered, "Werewolves, Mr. Wales."

Phil returned the glass back to the coffee table and sat there with his mouth gaped open. He looked at Joe and then at Claire, "You mean... like in the movies, werewolves?"

William stood from the recliner and walked over to Claire's side. Then he said, "Sure you don't want something a little stronger than that tea, son?"

Both Joe and Phil stared at William. Claire said, "This story cannot be made public. Imagine if everyone found out that ole Judge Jones' wife believed in werewolves. Not to mention that her family was somehow tied to this mythical creature… But I do believe that it's real. What do you think those things getting out the back of that truck were, gentlemen?"

Joe was the first to respond, "First off, William… I'm off duty right now, so I'm gonna take you up on that drink if you don't care." William turned to fix the drink as Joe turned to Claire and continued to speak, "Let me get this straight… You believe that Eva Mae and her sons have opened the bottle and possibly drank some of the contents?"

Claire answered, "Yes."

Then Phil asked, "What's in the bottle… besides evil?"

Claire responded, "Wine, plus whatever the Baron added. The bottles have been passed down through generations and eventually made their way to the United States with our father. Eva Mae and I were the next two who were given the task of guarding them. As you can see, my bottle is still intact. I don't believe the same can be said for Eva Mae's."

Phil stood and walked over to William at the cabinet bar. Softly he said, "Make me one of those also, Mr. Jones."

Then Phil turned back to Claire. She was still sitting in the chair, but now her eyes were staring at the floor. Phil spoke in a questioning tone, "Claire… so what we are saying here is, just like in the old horror films, a mad scientist that lived in an old castle on a hill above a village was somehow turning human beings into real, live werewolves. And these things were periodically preying on livestock in the surrounding area as they roamed the countryside. And now… through whatever the old Baron added to the wine in these bottles, they are walking and hunting here in the Southern Appalachians."

Claire slowly lifted her head and looked at Joe, who had never moved from his position on the couch. Then she replied, "I know it sounds crazy, gentlemen. Even my father didn't believe the story. He always said that our story was probably what sparked the entire werewolf craze, then he would laugh so hard that his belly would shake. After calming down, he would make fun of the fact that this was our family's legacy, but... he never broke the seal on either bottle. I think in the back of his mind, he too was a little fearful of the contents of the bottle."

William handed both glasses to Phil, who then ambled over to Joe and passed one of the glasses to his partner. Phil walked around Claire and returned to his seat on the couch. William returned to the recliner and sat down. Joe studied the contents of the glass for just a second, then he addressed William and his wife, "The person that recorded the film footage... Well, let's just say that he pursued some avenues prior to talking to us. Apparently, there have been several attacks on livestock, and their injuries are consistent with the five human victims. But like you stated at the courthouse, Mr. Jones... the attacks have occurred in a wide range of locations. How do we explain this?"

Claire was quick to answer, "The truck."

Phil took a long sip of the whiskey and paused as the burn in his throat dissipated. Then he asked, "You mean she's transporting them to different areas to hunt... like dogs?"

Claire replied, "Yes. Why else would they be in the back of the truck hidden under the camper top?"

Joe placed his hand onto his forehead and slowly rubbed the area above his eyebrows. After a short pause, he began to speak, "Do you people realize just what we are talking about here? I mean... we are talking about a mythical creature that terrified each and every one of us when we were young. The thought of such an animal stalking the darkness scared the living daylights out of me in my childhood days, but then I realized it was only mythical in nature. There were no such things as vampires and werewolves, not even in Transylvania. But now... we are talking about them like their existence is common knowledge."

Claire smiled at Joe. "I believe what I saw on that video is real, and so does the person that gave it to you. I'm hoping that, in time, you come to believe the story that I just conveyed to you guys. They have to be stopped, Mr. Wales."

Joe heavily sighed and asked, "How in the world are we going to prove that those things getting out of the truck are indeed werewolves? There's no way that I can just march into the office and tell the guys we got a couple of werewolves on the loose."

William responded with his own question, "What about the other incidents? Is there some way to talk to somebody about the other attacks?"

Joe took a glance at the clock on the wall, but he never took the time to focus on it. He then turned back to William and answered, "We have the names of the two rangers involved with the investigation of the hikers in the Great Smoky Mountains. I'll see if we can arrange a discreet meeting with the gentlemen."

"When did the attack take place in the Great Smoky Mountains?" asked Claire.

Phil responded, "In May of this year."

Claire turned to William, "They need to check Eva Mae's cellphone records... and the boys too. Just to confirm if the three of them were down there when the attacks occurred."

William responded, "I'll sign the paperwork, guys, if you can get it all in order. Let's just try to keep this as quiet as possible... You know, don't throw up any flags. We don't want people questioning what we are doing... not yet."

Both of the agents agreed and rose from their seats. They thanked the couple for the drinks and assured them they would get back to them with any information they acquired. Judge Jones and Claire thanked the agents for listening to the story of Claire's family, then the group said their goodbyes.

Joe climbed into the driver's seat and buckled the seatbelt. Phil followed suit on the passenger side of the truck. Joe turned the key, and the vehicle roared to life. Within a couple of minutes, the two men had navigated down the road completely out of site from the Jones' residence.

Joe pulled the truck into an empty parking lot for a local restaurant that had gone out of business. For reasons he wasn't sure of, Joe perfectly parked the vehicle in one of the spots that customers used when visiting the establishment. Joe placed the truck into park and switched off the key. He sat there staring out the front windshield.

Phil turned his head toward Joe and asked, "That was some story... Do you think this is really possible?"

Joe took a deep breath and replied, "She saw those things get out of the truck and go up the steps to the house. There didn't seem to be a lot of doubt in her mind."

Phil said, "The judge sure was hip on us talking to his wife when we were at the courthouse. Plus... he offered up getting the phone records rather easily."

Joe responded, "I think those two people are genuinely afraid of what they watched on that video."

"You think they are afraid of Claire's sister and the two boys?" asked Phil.

Joe answered, "Hard to say... Maybe they just don't want the family name destroyed, who knows. We'll get the phone records and see if these people were indeed in the Great Smoky Mountains in May. If so... we'll get ahold of the rangers and set up a meeting—very discreetly, though. We will kinda have to be careful with this werewolf thing. After all, I'm still trying to sort all of this out myself. I can only imagine trying to explain this to someone else without looking totally ridiculous."

Phil shook his head and replied, "Yeah... I agree. This whole thing has grown way out of proportion since the discovery of the victim on that ridge."

Joe grinned. "That could be the understatement of the year if these things are truly real. We'll see what the phone records say and take it one step at a time."

Phil nodded his head, and Joe started the truck. Once again, the men were traveling down the road. Each man sat silently, running the events of the incident and the story that Claire shared through their minds. Hopefully the phone records would be able to send the agents in some kind of positive direction.

CHAPTER 12

It only took a couple of days, and Joe had the cellphone records for Eva Mae and her two sons. He wasn't sure if he wanted the records to prove they were actually in the Great Smoky Mountains or if they were nowhere close to the park in May. Joe slowly scanned the information on the piece of paper until the moment the data jumped off the page it was typed on. Eva Mae made several calls from May 21st through May 25th. The calls had indeed pinged off the cell towers in and around Gatlinburg, Tennessee, and a quick check of the boys' phone records exhibited the same information.

Joe dropped his head as he tried to contemplate what their next move would be. Then he thought to himself, *How in the world does a man tell his superiors that they are chasing werewolves? How is a person supposed to stop these things from attacking? Are we going to try and capture them, or will we have to kill the creatures? Do we need silver bullets like depicted in the movies, or will a regular hollow point bullet do the trick?*

After a short pause, Joe looked across the room with a blank stare. He thought, "Good gosh... I'm acting like these mythical creatures do exist. There has to be a logical solution to this."

Joe picked up his phone and called Phil. After the second ring, Phil answered, "Hey, buddy... What's on your mind?"

Joe responded with a touch of sarcasm, "Whatever happened to just saying hello?"

Phil chuckled and replied, "I guess when we got these little phones, saved everybody's names and numbers so we would know who's calling, there's really no reason to answer the call in the old-fashioned way. So... what's up?"

Joe just shook his head in disbelief and answered, "Well... I guess I'm gonna make that call to the rangers. Records show that Eva Mae and her two sons were indeed in the Smokies in May, at the right time frame."

Phil paused for just a second and said, "I was kinda hoping that the phone records would be a dead end." Then he asked, "Joe, there really can't be such a thing as Claire described, can there?"

Joe answered, "I really don't think so, Phil. I'll make the call, and we'll go talk to the rangers. Maybe they can shed some light on the situation. I'll let you know if and when they want to meet."

Phil responded, "Sounds good, Joe. Just let me know."

Both men ended the calls on their phones, and Joe opened the desk drawer and removed the folded piece of paper that he had written Sonny Rutherford's number on. It had only taken a few minutes of Joe's time for the search to come up with Sonny's number using a funded site for state government employees. He had been hoping that the time it took to locate the number would turn out to be just a small waste of his time. But now Joe realized that pressing the digits on the small handheld device was something he had to do.

* * *

Sonny Rutherford had just twisted the cap off of a bottled water. He was watching the steady stream of vehicles passing the Sugarlands Visitor Center moving in both directions. The abrupt ringing of the phone had slightly caught Sonny off guard, evident by the small amount of water spilling from the top of the bottle as his body jerked. Sonny removed the phone from the pocket of the National Park-issued shirt; he studied the numbers displayed on the screen. Right away, he realized that he didn't recognize the number of the person calling and debated on answering. But curiosity got the cat, as they say, and Sonny swiped up on the phone to answer.

"Hello, this is Sonny Rutherford," he said.

The voice from the phone began to speak, "Mr. Rutherford, this is Joseph Wales. I'm a Tennessee Wildlife Resource Agent from upper East Tennessee. We had an incident at a local lake that seems to be quite similar to an event you guys had down there in the National Park. I was wondering if it would be possible for my partner and I to meet with you to discuss the cases."

Sonny asked, "What event are we talking about, Mr. Wales?"

"The incident where the two hikers were killed right above the visitor center," answered Joe.

Immediately, Sonny's interest was piqued, and he glanced around the area in front of the center and noticed several individuals either leaving or making their way into the building. Sonny then responded, "Give me just a second, Mr. Wales. I want to make sure nobody can hear our conversation."

Sonny walked away from the building to a large grassy area adjacent to the parking lot. Once alone, Sonny continued, "Mr. Wales, our case was closed by the state. I'm not sure I can offer up any more information than what's in the report."

Sonny was well aware there were other details to offer up but wasn't quite sure of when and how to release the information. But Joe helped the situation when he asked if he and Phillip could drive down and meet privately with him. Sonny glanced at the traffic once again and said, "Yes... Better to discuss things in person rather than over the phone."

Sonny was fishing a little about the meeting, and Joe picked up on it right away. Joe responded, "I agree, Mr. Rutherford. When would be a good time for us to get together?"

Sonny informed Joe that he would like to include his partner, plus there would be an additional two people at the meeting. He then assured Joe that the three people knew exactly what he did about the case. Hopefully between the four of them, no detail would be left out. Joe agreed, and the two men arranged a date and time for the meeting.

After hanging up, Sonny called Billy, Sarah, and Rhonda. He explained the call and informed them of the date and time for the meeting. Joe immediately called Phil and supplied him with all the information.

At 5:30 on Saturday afternoon, Rhonda pulled into Sonny and Sarah's driveway. Billy's truck was already parked beside Sarah's vehicle. Even though there was nobody there to hear her, Rhonda said, "Last to arrive again. At least I beat the TWRA guys."

Rhonda turned off the jeep and made her way to the front door. After two knocks, she heard footsteps approaching from the inside. Sarah opened the door with a smile and told Rhonda that the men were sitting at the dining room table. She then offered Rhonda some coffee and said they would wait for the other gentlemen to arrive before serving the pie.

Rhonda grinned and asked, "Apple pie?"

Sarah smiled. "Nope... This time, it's peach cobbler and vanilla ice cream."

Rhonda's eyes lit up as she said, "Oh yeah... That's another of my favorites."

Sarah closed the door and the two of them walked to the kitchen and dining room area. Both Sonny and Billy smiled as they welcomed Rhonda to the room. Rhonda slid out the only chair that remained tucked under the edge of the table. As she placed herself into the seat, Sarah placed the warm mug on the table next to Rhonda, who graciously thanked her.

Rhonda took a sip of the hot coffee and gently placed the cup back on the table. Then she looked at Sonny and asked, "So... do you think these guys are looking for answers, or are they gonna provide us with some answers?"

Sonny replied, "I couldn't tell from the phone conversation. I guess time will tell."

Phil then added, "They did want it to be a private meeting, though, right?"

Sonny nodded. "Yeah. What do you guys think about the hair? Do we offer up that information or not?"

Rhonda replied, "We'll just have to play that by ear."

Sonny nodded and responded, "We let you decide if and when to tell them about the hair."

Billy was the next to speak, "Speaking of the hair… your friend said that it had wolf characteristics."

Rhonda answered, "Yes… but no known match to any wolf in the data base."

Billy lifted his left hand and cupped his chin. Slowly he began to caress the stubble of hairs beginning to protrude from the skin. Then Billy spoke, "Listen… I've been doing a lot of thinking and searching, people." He looked Sonny directly in the eyes and asked, "How about your people's folklore, Chief?"

Sonny chuckled as Billy returned his hand to the table. "My people's folklore?" he repeated. "What in the world are you talking about, Billy?"

Billy grinned as he tilted his head slightly. "Just about every group of people have creatures or monsters that they talk about. What about the Cherokee Devil Dog or some kind of shape shifter creature? Maybe that's why this hair doesn't show up in any data base?"

Sonny laughed and said, "Well, I've never seen one of those things, Billy. But hey… why don't we throw bigfoot into the mix as well?"

"Wait a minute, Chief… The hair was wolf, not primate. Plus, I think that ole bigfoot may just really be out there," replied Billy.

Everybody at the table laughed, and Sarah said, "I didn't really picture you as a bigfoot enthusiast, Billy."

Billy grinned. "I never said enthusiast; I just said that maybe they are real."

Just then, the four people heard the slamming of the vehicle doors out in the driveway. Sonny grinned and pointed at Billy as he said, "Let's leave the ole Cherokee Devil Dog out of this until we see what these gentlemen have to say."

Billy nodded and laughed as Sonny slid his chair away from the table. Then Sonny disappeared from the room as he went to greet the two agents. The front door of the chalet-style house swung open just as Joe and Phil arrived at the base of the steps. Both men looked up as Sonny emerged from the house. Sonny smiled and greeted the men, "Sonny Rutherford... Guys, you must be Joseph and Phillip."

Both of the agents smiled as Joe responded, "Yes, sir... but let's just go with Joe and Phil."

Sonny grinned and said, "Sounds good. Come on in... My wife has made a peach cobbler, and I don't want any of it left over, guys. Heaven knows I don't want to be eating cobbler all week."

The men exchanged handshakes, and after closing the door Sonny led the agents into the dining room area. Sarah had already retrieved the two extra dining room chairs and placed them at the table. When the three men entered the room, Sarah, Billy, and Rhonda all stood to greet the agents. After the introductions were complete, everybody took a seat. Joe and Phil were seated next to each other. Sarah announced that she had enough pie and ice cream to feed a small army. She then asked Sonny to help serve.

As Sonny began to walk toward the kitchen, he pointed at the agents and said, "Remember what I said, boys..." Then Sonny shook his index finger and continued, "No pie left over."

Sarah laughed as she passed the kitchen counter. She stated, "Ole Sonny's afraid he'll be eating peach cobbler all week. Always worried about keeping that old man figure in check."

Sonny replied, "Kinda... but mostly afraid of the bears around here. If they smell peach cobbler on my breath and decide to chase me down, I'd like to be able to outrun them to the truck."

Rhonda was the next to speak, "Ah, Sonny... Just trip Billy and you won't be the slowest guy in the woods that day."

Billy grinned and responded, "Don't give Chief no ideas, Rhonda... and by the way, I kinda thought you and I were better friends than that."

Everybody laughed as Sonny and Sarah started delivering the pie and ice cream to the table. Then the two coffee mugs were set in front of the agents, and everyone's cup was filled. Both Joe and Phil had already suspected that Sonny was part Indian, which confirmed their suspicions when Billy had referred to him as Chief. There wasn't much conversation as the group consumed the pie and ice cream. Billy and Phil both asked for seconds. Sonny laughed and told the younger guys to just wait; there would come a time that a second helping of pie would become harder and harder to work off. After finishing the dessert, everybody complemented Sarah on the pie.

Just as Sonny was going to begin the meeting, Joe's phone came to life and started ringing. Joe removed the device from his shirt pocket and studied the number. He looked at Phil and said, "Roger."

The other people just stared at the agents when Phil replied, "Better answer it... Maybe he's got some information for us."

Joe answered the call, "Hello."

Roger's voice transmitted through the small device, "Joe, this is Roger... Can you talk?"

Joe glanced around the table. Phil nodded yes. Both men had already gotten pretty comfortable with the four people they had just met. He decided to remain at the table while taking the call from Roger. Joe replied, "Yes, what's up?"

Roger then informed Joe, "I believe there's been another attack... down in the Nolichucky River Basin."

Joe glanced at Phil and asked, “Another one?”

“Yes, on July the 21st. A couple was attacked at their horse barn behind the house,” answered Roger.

Then Joe started to ask, “Were they...”

Roger interrupted, “No... both survived. They were roughed up a bit, bruises and lacerations. But from what I can gather, the family’s pets saved the couple’s lives. Each of the victims fired a couple of shots at the creatures, but none of them connected.”

Joe then asked, “Did they give a description of the creatures to the authorities?”

Roger cleared his throat and answered, “Well, as a matter of fact, the couple are being a little tightlipped about whatever it was that attacked them.”

Joe rubbed the back of his head and said, “Yeah, imagine that.”

Roger explained, “I think they saw a lot more than they are talking about. Apparently, the attack was lengthy enough for the couple to at least get a glimpse of the creatures. For crying out loud, they both fired shots at them, and the dogs had to run from the house to the barn after the attack started.”

Joe took a deep breath and exhaled the air, “What makes you think it’s the same creatures?”

Roger answered with confidence, “The dogs... One of them grabbed a creature by the arm as it was attacking the husband; the other dog bit the second creature on the leg. There may have been other successful strikes by the dogs, but I’m not totally sure. Maybe more information is available in the official report. And Joe... Ellen and I saw the boys sitting on the front porch with their mother. We could see a bandage on Ronnie’s arm and one on Ricky’s leg with the binoculars, but we made sure that nobody saw us looking. Plus, we got film footage to prove it.”

Joe rubbed his eyes and replied, “Okay, thanks, Roger. Phil and I are meeting with the park rangers tonight." Then Joe looked around the table at everyone and continued, "Don't let anyone find out that you are recording the activity at that house. Phil and I will get together with you guys next week. We've got some information to share with you. Maybe this meeting with the rangers can give us some added information. I'll call and we'll get together."

Both men ended the calls on their phones. Joe placed his cellphone on the table and stared at the screen until it went dark.

CHAPTER 13

When Joe looked up, everybody at the table was staring directly at him. Then he looked at Phil and said, "It appears that another attack has taken place, down next to the Nolichucky River at a couple's farm. But both people survived this time. However, they're not being very descriptive to the authorities about whatever it was that attacked them."

Phil asked, "How do we know this attack was perpetrated by the same things as our victims at the lake?"

Rhonda was quick to interrupt before Joe could answer, "You said things... plural."

Next to chime in was Sonny, "And what makes you guys believe that our incident here in the Smokies is related to the attack you investigated?"

Joe leaned back in his chair and paused for a second, then decided to lay all the cards on the table. Methodically he began to speak, "We were notified on the night of June the 21st that two local fishermen had found a woman floating in a bass boat all alone. The woman appeared to be in some state of shock. She didn't offer much information as to what exactly had occurred. As a matter of fact, it seemed that the events of the night were somehow mentally blocked out of her mind. I really don't know if we will ever get much information out of her. The doctors seem to think the same thing."

Joe took a deep breath and continued, "After we got her back to the boat ramp and the help we requested arrived, we started to investigate the scene. The investigation led us to believe that whoever was in the boat with her was pulled out the craft and dragged up a steep incline to the top of the ridge. Turned out, this person was the woman's husband. When we found the man, his internal organs were missing."

Billy looked Joe in the eyes and said, "Just like our two hikers."

Joe responded, "Yes... just like the hikers. Listen, people. Whatever dragged this man up that hill was definitely pretty strong."

Rhonda was the next to speak, "Did anyone find any kind of evidence as to what the attacker was?"

Phil answered, "No... nothing was found at the scene. Was there something found down here?"

Rhonda decided to play one of her high cards now. "Yes. We found a hair in the chest cavity of one of the victims. The state first off said it was of unknown origin but later labeled it as the hair of a black bear. They notified the families and closed the case."

Joe raised his eyebrows and stated, "Pretty quick on the closure, wouldn't you say?"

Then Sonny spoke, "We were notified that the case was closed. But I'm telling you... if there had been a rogue bear roaming in the park, it would have been a full-on search for the animal."

Then Joe continued, "Since that night in June, Phil and I have been in a whirlwind of strange information. As far as we can tell both... both of our informants are very creditable people. There are spouses involved also, but everyone wants to remain anonymous, so all of this has been kinda dumped into our laps."

Rhonda sensed the uneasiness in Joe's voice and decided to play her next high card to hopefully add some reassurance to him, "We found a second hair at the couple's campsite. Sarah spotted it clinging to a small sapling. I gave it to a personal friend to analyze. That person came back with some interesting information. The best that could be determined was that the hair contained wolf characteristics, but to no known wolf in the United States, or anywhere in the world for that matter."

Phil turned to Joe and asked, "Holy mackerel... Do you think Claire is right?"

Everyone stared at Joe as he caressed his forehead with the fingers of his right hand. Joe dropped his hand and chuckled, then looked at the group and said, "First off... Phil and I are very sane individuals. I'm gonna go through the details from the first informant and his wife, then I'm gonna tell you a family story from the second informant and her husband. These people's names and professions cannot be shared with anyone at any time." Joe looked at Rhonda and continued, "Exactly the same way that you don't want to share your friend's name."

Joe looked around the table at each individual, and all nodded in agreement. First, he explained meeting Roger, the deputy, at the scene on South Holston Lake. Joe then described the night that he and Phil met Roger and Ellen at their house; no details were left out. Joe informed the group that they had brought the thumb drive with them, and everybody was welcome to view it when he finished.

Next, Joe told the group about the meeting with Judge Jones and the reaction he had to the film footage. After a deep breath, Joe explained Claire's family history—everything from the village in Transylvania to present time. For the entire time that Joe was talking, he was staring at the center of the table. The others simply watched him as he talked—all except Phil, who gripped his coffee cup with both hands while listening to the elaborate story of their adventure so far.

There was a small moment of silence that filled the room, then Joe looked at Phil and asked, "Did I miss anything?"

Phil turned loose of the cup and leaned back in his chair. "No, sir... I'm pretty sure that's everything."

Joe shifted his eyes toward Sonny and said, "I know this is a pretty wild story... There's got to be a logical explanation for all this."

Billy picked up his phone from the table and swiped up to open the apps. He looked at Joe and asked, "So, do we have a date on the two deer hunters above Damascus, Virginia, that Roger was talking about?"

Joe answered, "No, just that it was during the hunting season last year. I suppose with a little research we could come up with an exact date."

Sonny then addressed Joe, "So what we are saying is that we have five individuals with the same injuries. Two above Damascus, Virginia; one at South Holston Reservoir; and the two here in the Smoky Mountains."

Joe simply replied, "Yes."

Then Phil added, "Plus the attacks on livestock in various locations... but we don't have exact dates on them either."

Then Rhonda asked, "What about the phone call?"

Joe shrugged and answered, "Well, that was Roger, and according to what he believes... whatever killed those five people also attacked a couple along the Nolichucky River."

Sarah slid her chair back, placed both hands on the table, and stood to her feet. She walked over to the kitchen counter and turned to lean against it. Then she asked, "What makes Roger think that this attack along the river is the same creatures?"

Joe shifted his eyes to look at Sarah before answering, "The couple had two dogs... Each of the creatures was bitten by a dog. One on the arm and another on the leg. That's all the couple relayed to the investigators during the report. Maybe there were more strikes by the dogs, but that's the only two that we know for sure."

Rhonda then asked, "But what is the significance of the two dog bites?"

Joe grinned. "Well... Eva Mae's sons had bandages on them: one on the arm and one on the leg."

Just then, Billy interrupted, "What was the date of the attack on the Nolichucky River?"

"Roger said it was July the 21st," answered Joe.

Billy swiped the screen on the phone to the right, back to the left, and then right again. He looked at the group and said, "The ole judge's wife might just know what she's talking about."

Rhonda asked, "What in the world are you talking about, Billy?"

Billy smiled and replied, "The attack here and the attack at the lake have more in common than just the internal organs, plus the deer hunter attack in Virginia kinda falls in the right timeline. The attack along the river is spot on with the Smoky Mountains and South Holston Lake."

Then Sonny asked Billy, "What do you mean?"

Billy pointed to his phone and answered, "The three dates that we do have are on a full moon. The hunters are quite possibly in that exact timeline last year. There was a full moon during the hunting season also. That incident may very well have occurred on that date. Just like the old horror flicks, people, we may be looking for a couple of werewolves in this investigation."

Sonny laughed and said, "Five minutes before the agents arrived, you were making fun of my people's folklore–the Cherokee Devil Dog and shape shifters. Now you're telling me that werewolves from Transylvania killed these people. All these attacks have occurred in distinctively different areas; how do we account for that?"

Phil turned his head toward Sonny and answered, "Claire thinks that her sister is transporting the boys to different areas to hunt, like dogs. And unfortunately, the three of them were in Gatlinburg when the attack happened here; their cellphones pinged on the towers in and around the area."

Rhonda asked if they could view the video that Roger and Ellen had recorded, and Sarah said she would get the laptop from the living room. Everyone sat silently, trying to process all the information that had been presented. Only Billy was actively moving at all. He was swiping the phone screen left and right, confirming the dates of the full moon. He established in his mind that he was indeed correct on the dates of the attacks and the full moons. Sarah returned to the dining room with the computer in her hands, and she placed it on the table in front of Joe.

Joe looked at Sonny and asked, "You want the honors?"

Sonny smiled and answered, "I hate those things... I might actually erase the video accidently before we even get to watch it. Maybe you better operate that thing."

Joe laughed, "Okay, people... Gather around for the movie."

Joe opened the computer as everyone stood and walked behind him to take their position. He removed the flash drive from his pocket and inserted it into the machine. Within a few seconds after striking a couple of keys, the video appeared on the screen. Everyone except Phil, who remained seated, watched the computer intently as the video began to play. Nobody said a word as the truck pulled into the driveway; they continued to watch the screen as Eva Mae exited the truck and walked to the house. Once she opened the front door, they all watched the woman make her way back to the vehicle. Next, they witnessed Eva Mae lifting the camper top cover and lowering the tailgate.

Nothing prepared the park rangers, Rhonda, and Sarah for what they viewed next. They leaned closer to the table as the two creatures exited the back of the truck and scurried into the house through the front door. Each and every person took notice of the second creature traversing the steps on its hind legs before dropping back to all fours as it entered the house. Even without being asked, Joe immediately played the video a second time. All four people plus Joe watched the footage again.

The group stood there somewhat dumbfounded. Billy finally broke the silence, "Did you people see the second animal going up the steps?"

Sonny turned and walked back to his seat. He sat down and addressed the others, "Okay... I've seen some strange animal behavior before, but I have never seen anything like that. Those two things were pretty big guys, and it only took a couple of seconds for them to exit the truck and disappear into the house." Then Sonny looked at Joe and asked, "What do you and Phil make of this video?"

Phil shook his head and Joe stared at Sonny with a blank facial expression. Finally, Joe answered, "I'd like to think there is a logical explanation for all of this. Problem is... I can't come up with one."

Then Sonny asked, "Have you mentioned this to any of your bosses... or any other investigative agencies?"

Joe grinned and replied, "Not a chance, Sonny... I kinda want to keep my job."

Rhonda was next to raise a question to the group, "What do we do now?"

Billy then spoke, "I don't know if we are all on the same page or not, people, but if Claire is right... there's another full moon on August the 19th. That's just a few days until there could be another attack."

Sonny looked at Billy and then at every person in the room. Then he asked, "So... are we admitting to each other that these creatures that terrified our childhood days are indeed real? Are we saying that we honestly believe in werewolves?"

Rhonda responded, "I think we are, Sonny. The analysis of the hair by Angie..." She paused. It was the first time that she had named her friend. Then Rhonda continued, "...the video, the story of the wine and Claire's family heritage... Everything is pointing to the same conclusion."

Billy grinned and said, "At least it's not the ole Cherokee Devil Dog, Sonny."

Sonny laughed and shook his head. "I don't know, Billy. That might just be a little easier to explain than this."

Joe removed the flash drive and placed it back into his pocket. Next he powered down the computer. As he closed the lid on the device, he addressed the others, "Let Phil and I see if we can have an off-the-record conversation with the couple down on the river. If we are up front and honest with them, maybe they'll share a little more information with us. We are also going to let Roger and Ellen show us the video of the boys sitting on the porch. Let's just keep tonight's meeting between us. If we find out anything, I'll holler at you, Sonny. Heck, if we don't find out any new information, I'll still holler at you. We need to figure out exactly what we are going to do."

Sonny responded, "We would appreciate it, Joe. We'll help in any way we can."

Joe grinned. "Don't forget that you said that; we may just need some backup in our neck of the woods."

Sonny stated, "That would be out of our jurisdiction, Mr. Wales."

Joe laughed and replied, "There's no such thing as jurisdiction when chasing mythical creatures."

Everybody laughed, and the two TWRA agents thanked Sarah for the dessert. Soon the two men were on their way back to Sullivan County, Tennessee, and Billy and Rhonda left to return to their homes. Sonny helped Sarah clean up, and the two of them retired for the night. Sleep did not come easy for any of the four people residing in the Great Smoky Mountain area. The events of the evening ran through their minds as they tossed and turned.

CHAPTER 14

The morning began in the normal routine for Roger and Ellen. Letting the dogs out was the first in their ritual. Both Ben and Jerry scurried through the front door and traveled down the porch steps; each was in search of the perfect tree to relieve themselves from the long night's sleep. Roger's next move was to start the coffee brewing. Ellen removed the bacon and eggs from the fridge. Roger grabbed a can of biscuits and peeled the wrapper from the can, and just as he pressed on the magic spot, the dogs came running back into the house. With the ole familiar popping sound, the can opened, and Roger began placing the biscuits onto the bread pan.

As Ellen crossed the living room to close the door, she noticed Eva Mae walking toward her truck from out the window. She closed the door, walked over to the window, and watched the activity next door. Then she said, "Roger... looks like the neighbors may be going on a little trip. Eva Mae and the boys have suitcases in hand."

Roger turned to Ellen and asked, "Are you sure?"

Ellen answered, "I'm pretty sure... They put the suitcases in the back of the truck and all three of them got into the cab of the truck. They're backing out right now... Maybe it's just a weekend trip."

Just then, Roger's phone began to ring. He glanced at the screen and answered, "Joe, we may have a problem."

Joe was caught off guard by the way Roger answered the phone. He was expecting the normal reply of "hello." After regaining his composure, Joe responded, "What's the matter, Roger?"

Roger explained what Ellen had just witnessed at Eva Mae's house. Then he said, "It's almost been a month since the attack on the Nolichucky River."

Joe glanced at the calendar sitting on his desk, then replied, "Yes, it has... and two days from now, we have a full moon."

Roger asked, "A full moon?"

Joe responded, "Yeah, Roger... We have gathered a lot of strange information since we last met. I'd rather not talk about it over the phone. Can Phil and I come over for a visit tonight?"

Roger looked at Ellen and replied, "How about 7:30 tonight?"

Joe answered, "Sounds good... See you then."

Both men ended the calls on their phones. Roger informed Ellen that Joe and Phil were coming over tonight. Ellen grinned with excitement. Then Roger mentioned the comment that Joe made about the full moon. He walked over to the calendar hanging on the dining room wall. He removed the calendar from the small nail it was hanging on and started flipping through the pages. First, he looked at the date of the attack in the Smokies. Next was the date that the man was killed on South Holston Lake. Lastly, he thumbed the pages to find the date of the attack at the Nolichucky River. Roger turned to face Ellen and informed her that all three attacks occurred during a full moon phase, then he returned the calendar to display the current month as all the thoughts raced through his mind.

Roger exclaimed, "Oh no... August the 19th is a full moon, Ellen. That's just two days from now. Wonder where Eva Mae and the boys are going?"

* * *

It was early that same Saturday morning when the group of young people met on the outskirts of Maggie Valley, North Carolina. One by one, they arrived at the designated spot to start the extended weekend adventure. Every couple of months, the group would assemble to hike and explore the surrounding mountains, spending three or four nights camping in the wilderness. Normally there were seven young adults ranging from 25 to 29 years of age. However, Emma had to opt out of this excursion. She had been under the weather with a mild case of the flu and was afraid of the effects the hike may subject her to. After she had returned to work that week, she informed two of the people that she probably should sit this one out, but hopefully she could participate in the next adventure.

The six members of their little club gathered all of their gear and departed the parking area. This particular adventure was one that the group embarked on at least once a year; they would hike most of the day until their destination on top of the mountain was achieved.

Brian, Donna, Alex, Rita, Cliff, and Frank began the trek to the abandoned amusement park at the top of the mountain. What once was a thriving source of entertainment for all ages now lay empty—a ghostly reminder of days gone by nestled amongst the trees. "Ghost Town in the Sky" had been the name of the park. Grown adults from all around had fond memories of their visits to this magical park as children.

The six individuals slowly made their way through the winding foot trails on their quest of the mountain. Each kept thinking of what a nice break it would be to camp in the old Western-style town, and to forget about work for a few days and nights. There was plenty of exploration to do around the old amusement park. And if the weather was to suddenly take a turn for the worse, there were plenty of places to take refuge amongst the old buildings.

The group made their way along the familiar trail that crisscrossed the valleys and ridges of the mountains of the area. Just about noon, they finally intersected the trail for the ascent to the top of the mountain where the old amusement park now lay abandoned. After a short rest to relieve their bodies from the weight of the backpacks and to consume some much-needed hydration, the group continued their assault on the mountain. Everyone was elated to be away from the daily grinds of life. The stress of the climb and the weight of the gear was a welcomed burden to each of the hikers.

Every little bit, Brian, who was leading this little expedition, would pause and verbally question the group, "Everybody doin' okay?"

All would answer in a positive voice as they continued to suck in the fresh mountain air. Then after a brief pause, the group would methodically once again start placing one foot in front of the other in their quest of the mountain. There was plenty of wildlife to observe as they trekked along. The birds were zipping from tree limb to tree limb. A mother deer and her two fawns born earlier at the beginning of summer crossed the trail. They simply ambled through the forest adjacent to the hikers for several minutes. The young fawns kept a curious eye on the hikers as they moved along. A large black bear was spotted on the side of the mountain digging in an old fallen log, no doubt looking for some grubs to make an easy meal of. No manmade sounds were audible to the group other than the sounds that the six people were making as they trekked along.

After a few hours, the group broke through the trees to the area at the top of the mountain that the abandoned facility called home. The area had an eeriness to it, the old wooden buildings still standing at the spot where the old Wild West gunfight shows would take place. It almost had the appearance of the vacated Western towns that one would watch on television in one of those old haunted shows. That is, until the semi-modern skeletons of the many amusement thrill rides came into view and a person would once again remember just where they really were.

Everybody walked up, even with Brian, and stared into the old park. Then Brian asked the group, "How about we set up camp right at the end of the old town?"

Alex was the first to respond, "Sounds good... That was a good spot the last time we were here."

"Yeah, buddy. That's where all the ole ghosts hang out, right in the old town," Rita added.

The entire group laughed. Then Donna said, "Don't you people start that ghost stuff, or somebody can escort me back down the mountain."

Frank patted Donna on the shoulder and said, "If we have an encounter with a ghost, I'll be more than happy to escort you back to the car. Just make sure you can keep pace with me."

The group of six individuals then walked up to the edge of the old Western-style buildings that made up the town. Then Cliff said, "Doesn't look like anyone has been up here since the last time we were here."

Rita snickered, "Just the ghosts, but they don't leave footprints as they move between the buildings."

Donna turned to Rita and asked, "What's with all the ghost stuff?" Then she added, "We've not been here 10 minutes and you're already trying to put me on edge."

Rita laughed and replied, "I'm just poking fun at you. You're the one that said you thought this place was a little spooky after the last trip up here."

Donna grinned. "I do... but there's no need for you to keep reminding me about ghosts."

Once again, the six people all laughed, and Cliff said, "Come on, people. Let's get camp set up. I'm exhausted from the hike." Then he looked at Donna and said, "Ghost or no ghost, I'm ready to relax by the fire tonight."

Donna smiled and shook her head. Everybody walked up to the edge of the dusty ole street where the make-believe gunfights would take place. There, at the beginning of the town, was the circular formation of rocks for the group's firepit from the previous adventure to the park. Nothing appeared to have changed very much since their last visit; the bushes and trees that had started to reclaim the area had grown somewhat. And the vines that ran along the ground were stretching forth to new heights on the machinery and buildings as they climbed upwards. But the firepit and the surrounding area didn't show any signs of human interference; only a few bear tracks were visible in the dirt.

Everyone removed their backpacks and began to prepare the campsite. Each one of them set up their single-person tents and arranged the supplies they had brought. Once everybody was situated, the group collectively set up the rope pulley system to hoist their ready-to-eat food packages high into the air near one of the buildings. Nobody wanted to defend their food supplies with a hungry bear, especially in the dark.

Brian, Alex, Cliff, and Frank searched around for firewood while Donna and Rita readied the firepit. Cliff and Frank also found three good-sized logs for the six people to share as seats while they enjoyed the evening. Even though it was the middle of August, the nights ran a possibility of becoming a little chilly, especially if one of the frequent thunderstorms arose on the mountain.

Everyone ate one of the meals that night around the campfire that they had toted up the mountain. Mixed with a little water and heated over the open campfire, they produced a meal fit for any level of hiker out in the wilderness. They all sat around the campfire, laughed, and told stories. Some of the stories were from childhood days and some were from past experiences they had endured from earlier excursions. After a couple of hours, the exhaustion of the day's activities began to sink in, and collectively the group called it a night and retired to the comfort of their sleeping bags in the tents. In just a few minutes, they were all sound asleep under the millions of stars that littered the night sky.

* * *

Shortly after noon that day while the hikers were still climbing the mountain, Eva Mae positioned the turn signal to exit the interstate. At the bottom of the ramp, she turned right and headed toward Maggie Valley, North Carolina. In no time at all, the three people in the truck could see the sign welcoming them to the area. Not a tremendous amount had changed in this community since the time that the amusement park was a major attraction.

The quaint motels and eateries still bordered the road in the same manner they always had; a person could leave the worries of modern days behind to step back in time and enjoy a peaceful weekend. Just a little down the road from the parking area for the chairlift ride to the old "Ghost Town in the Sky" park, Eva Mae made the right turn onto the little road. Shortly, the truck crossed the bridge over the stream, and they entered the parking lot of the small, two-story motel that bordered the trees.

Eva Mae placed the truck into park and turned off the engine. She told the boys to sit tight, and she would be back in a couple of minutes. The boys were already starting to feel the effects of the changes that their bodies would be going through in a couple of days. They sat silently for the first couple of minutes, then Ricky asked, "It's gonna happen again, isn't it, Ronnie?"

Ronnie never quit staring out the windshield as he answered, "Yes... I believe so, Ricky."

Ricky asked, "Do you remember anything?"

Ronnie replied, "If you mean while we are monsters... no. But I can remember as we start to transform, and then when we are returning to normal once again."

Ricky dropped his head to look at the floorboard of the vehicle and said, "That's all I can remember too. I don't really know what happens between the rise of the moon and the dawn of the next morning... but I don't think what we do in the darkness is a good thing, Ronnie."

Ronnie turned to face Ricky, with a tear escaping the corner of his eye.

He replied, "I don't think so, Ricky. You know the family story as well as I do. I'm not sure what the outcome of this will be. I don't know if there's help for us or not. The story is true, and now this curse has been laid into our laps. I don't understand the 'why' of this situation or the reasoning of Mom. We may have to figure this out on our own."

After Eva Mae paid cash for the next four nights and registered under another name, she simply walked out of the office. She strolled across the parking lot to the truck and opened the door. Next, she informed the boys that they were set for the next four nights. The boys simply smiled at Eva Mae as she closed the door and started the truck. She asked Ronnie and Ricky about the kind of food they wanted for dinner, just like a mother would question her children on a weekend getaway. Both boys knew this was not just a getaway trip for the family; just by the way their bodies were beginning to feel, they realized that something bad was about to take place.

Soon, the trio finished eating and returned to the motel to relax. The boys tried to watch a ballgame on TV, but the wondering about what would take place in a couple of days occupied the minds of the youngsters as they laid on the king-size bed with their feet facing the television. Shortly, the tiredness overtook their bodies, and the boys faded off to sleep. Eva Mae stared at the boys sleeping on the bed until she nodded off in the chair.

CHAPTER 15

At 7:25, Joe and Phil parked the truck in the driveway at Roger's house, and both men climbed the steps. Phil rang the doorbell. In just a matter of seconds, the front door opened, and the agents were greeted with the smile on Ellen's face. She cordially invited the men inside and offered them something to drink. Joe opted for water and Phil chose a glass of sweet tea. Phil took a seat on the couch and Joe rested himself in the comforts of the large rocking chair.

Ellen sat on the couch next to Phil. As Roger sat in the recliner, he asked, "We can hardly wait... What's all this new information you spoke about?"

Phil replied, "Oh... this is some story, guys."

Then Joe began to explain about the meeting with Judge William Jones and his reaction to the film. He proceeded to explain how the judge wanted the two of them to meet with his wife, Claire. Joe took a deep breath and gave a detailed rendition of the family story that Claire had presented to them at the couple's home. Both Roger and Ellen intently stared at Joe as he spoke each and every word; neither of them dared interrupt as Joe walked through the events at William and Claire's home.

The next thing that Joe presented was the meeting at Sonny Rutherford's house with the four individuals from the Great Smoky Mountain area. Joe emphasized the fact that the state did not return the hair sample and how quickly they closed the case at the park. Next, he told Roger and Ellen about the second hair that the group found, and the analysis delivered by Rhonda's friend.

After Joe finished relaying all the details, he looked up at Roger, who smiled and said, "Now I know what the full moon comment was all about."

Phil chuckled and said, "I told you this was some story."

Ellen asked, "I know we all watched the video... but are we really talking about werewolves, people?" Then she stood from the couch and looked at Phil. "Is it really possible for something in that bottle to transform the two boys into monsters?"

Phil turned to Joe for support, then Joe replied, "That's kinda the same feeling we all had down at the park ranger's house. But I'm telling you, Claire told the story with conviction. There's no doubt that she believes the story that has been passed down through the generations, and I believe that her husband, William, believes the story to be true."

Then Roger spoke, "After we hung up, I did some searching on the calendar. All the attacks occurred during a full moon. I'm not totally sure about the deer hunters, but the other attacks took place during that phase of the moon. Oh, and by the way, two days from now will be another full moon, people. If Claire is right, then maybe they left the area to go on another hunt."

Phil nodded and replied, "That may indeed be the case. Problem is... we don't know where they went."

Ellen clutched the top of her shirt with her right hand and slowly caressed the material with two fingers, then said, "Unfortunately time will tell... We'll have to wait and see."

Then Roger asked, "We can't just tell everyone that we are chasing mythical werewolves from Transylvania, so how are we going to stop these things?"

Joe answered, "Quite a dilemma, wouldn't you say?"

Ellen slowly sat back onto the couch and asked, "So what is our next move?"

Joe sighed and answered, "We want you guys to kinda keep an eye out across the street. See when they come home and how the three of them act upon their arrival, but don't get caught spying, for crying out loud. Phil and I are going to see if the couple down on the Nolichucky River will open up to us a little more than they did to the investigators."

Roger rubbed the back of his neck. He said, "We should be able to catch them with the cameras even if we are not home. Hopefully the couple that survived can give us a little more information."

The group called it a night, and Joe and Phil exited the driveway. Both men took a long look at the dark house across the street as they started down the road. Neither man spoke as they traveled away from the edge of Holston Mountain toward town; it was a quiet ride with both men wondering about the whereabouts of Eva Mae and the two boys.

* * *

About two o'clock the next day, Joe and Phil pulled into the driveway at Shawn and Abby's house. It was one of those hot and lazy Sunday afternoons. There was no breeze blowing and the air was thick enough to cut with a knife—at least, that was the expression that some of the old timers that had spent their entire lives in the area would use from time to time. The men could clearly hear the couple's dogs barking from within the house as they approached the front steps. Suddenly the door opened, and Abby asked the men if she could help them.

Both men looked up at the door from where the sidewalk met the steps. Joe replied, "Yes, ma'am, if possible, we would like to talk to you and your husband about the incident you guys experienced the other night."

Abby bit her bottom lip slightly and responded, "We've already explained everything with the investigators. I really don't think there's much more to add."

Then Abby noticed that the men weren't sporting any kind of uniforms;

both men had surmised that the best way to go about this was in casual clothing. Hopefully the couple would be more cooperative if they felt this was just a casual conversation. Abby asked, "Who are you guys?"

Phil answered, "I'm Phil Weaver, and this is Joe Wales. We are TWRA agents, and we believe the same things that attacked you and your husband killed a fisherman on South Holston Lake back in June."

Joe added, "Ma'am, this is by no means an official visit. We are just hoping you guys might share some information that could possibly help us. We have some interesting information to share with you. We also have a video that we would like for both of you to watch... but we would like for the information and the video to remain secret."

Joe and Phil removed their badges and presented them to Abby. After studying the badges, Abby sighed and held up her index finger for the agents to wait there. She stepped back into the house and in just a minute returned to the door. Next, she invited the men inside. Both men graciously thanked her, and Phil took hold of the screen door. After Joe passed by him, Phil followed them into the house.

Shawn simply held up his hand slightly and welcomed the men. Right away, Joe and Phil realized why Shawn didn't make an effort to stand as the men entered the living room of the house. He was wrapped in medical gauze from under his armpits down to the top of the red sweatpants he wore. The chair was reclined to the position that Shawn's legs were resting on the footrest, and his house shoes were facing the television across the room. There was a baseball game taking place on the screen, but the volume was too low to hear the voices of the announcers. The agents weren't sure if the couple had been watching the game in this manner or if Shawn had turned down the volume before the men walked in.

Joe and Phil took seats on the couch and Abby offered them something to drink. Both men graciously declined. Then Joe said, "We're really sorry to bother you guys... but we were hoping you two could possibly help us a little."

Shawn responded, "I really don't know of anything we might have left out in our report to the investigators."

Phil looked at Joe and then back at Shawn. Abby was standing beside the recliner that Shawn was resting in. Then Phil said, "We were hoping that maybe you remembered some new detail... Maybe what your attackers looked like."

Abby laid her hand on Shawn's shoulder and stated, "Neither of us got a good look at them. It was pretty dark at the barn that night."

Then Joe said, "Listen... we have a pretty good idea what you guys were facing that night. I promise you, this conversation goes no further than this room. This is not some interrogation, and no report will be filed containing what any of us say." Joe tapped the top of the laptop computer he had carried with him. "Would you guys watch a video for us?"

Shawn turned his head to look at Abby, then focused back on the agents. "Sure... We'll take a look at it."

Joe opened the laptop and inserted the flash drive. When the file was opened, he stood and walked over to the recliner. Shawn took the computer and placed it in his lap. Next he tapped the "play" icon, and both people watched the screen. Joe continued to stand beside the foot of the recliner and observe the couple as they watched the video. There was no emotion displayed on their faces until the creatures exited the back of the truck; at that moment, both individuals leaned a little forward and slightly squinted their eyes.

Just as the second creature traversed the steps on its hindlegs, Abby gasped. As she squeezed Shawn's shoulder, she said, "That's exactly what that thing done up at the barn when it was running toward the woods. That's what I was explaining to you when we got back home, Shawn."

Then Joe asked, "So... you did kinda get a pretty good look at these things?"

Shawn answered, "Abby got a better look than I did. Everything happened so fast, guys. About all I saw was large, dark figures moving around in the night. By the time I could aim the flashlight, they were gone. I really don't recall much after the attack started; I just knew that I was fighting for my life."

Abby asked, "Where did you get this video? I mean, it's not fake, is it? You're not just trying to trick us into answering your questions, are you? We were nice enough to invite—"

Joe interrupted, "No, ma'am, the video is real. It appears that several attacks have occurred involving these creatures, but you two are the only ones that have been lucky enough to survive."

Abby said, "Sorry... I didn't mean to jump to conclusions. This entire experience has made me a little unnerved. I don't believe we would have survived if it weren't for the dogs. I knew there was no way I could give a description of what I saw that night." Then she smiled and asked, "Can you imagine what the investigators would have thought if I had given them a clear description of those things?"

Phil leaned forward on the couch and asked Abby, "So, you got a real good look at them?"

Abby smiled and replied, "Oh yeah." Then she pointed to the laptop, "The things that I saw up at the barn... Well, they looked and moved exactly like whatever that was that got out the back of that truck."

Shawn handed the computer back to Joe, who walked back over to the couch and removed the flash drive from the unit. As Joe sat down, Shawn asked, "What are those things?"

Both Phil and Joe adjusted themselves on the couch, then Phil asked, "What if we said they were a mythical creature from a long time ago?"

Abby said, "How about you name this so-called mythical creature, and then I tell you what I think I saw with the flashlight just before I fired the gun—just as the dog lunged at it, and as the creatures ran off?"

Joe took a deep breath and replied, "I don't know if you are gonna believe this or not, but we have reason to believe that what attacked you guys were werewolves."

Abby walked over to the door and stared toward the barn. Then she began to speak, "Ever since that night I've been trying to make some sense of what happened up there. I've tried to convince myself that what I saw was a bear or maybe a mountain lion, but I know what I saw. These two things were massive; their bodies and muscles were well defined. Their faces and heads were much larger than wolves, yet that was the shape that my brain deciphered that night. They were growling and snarling the entire time that the attack was occurring. They could move faster than a human being could react."

After a short pause, Abby turned to face the agents and continued, "I told Shawn that they looked just like the werewolves depicted in the movies... not the old movies, but some of the newer versions. I've never been that scared in my life. I still can't go out of this house in the dark, guys. We discussed everything from that night when we got home from the hospital, and we both decided it would be best if we just kept it to ourselves."

Joe asked Abby to have a seat, and he started from the beginning and explained everything to the couple. He told them about all the attacks and Claire's story of the family history, but he never mentioned anyone's name. Joe informed the couple that all involved were trying to remain anonymous, and that so far, he and Phil had been the common denominator to all the others. He assured the couple that their conversation that day would remain confidential, that the only part he might mention was the fact that they assisted in confirming the identity of the attackers.

The couple thanked the agents. Then Abby asked, "So... these creatures are real? You're telling us you believe?"

Joe took another deep breath and answered, "I've had a hard time grasping this idea of a real-life werewolf, but you know what you saw up there at the barn. All we had was this video—that is, until today. I believe you, Abby, and yes... I now believe these things are real."

Abby slightly raised her eyebrows and asked, "What now?"

Phil stood from the couch and said, "Somehow, we got to stop them."

As Joe stood from the couch, Shawn asked, "Can you keep us informed?"

Joe nodded and replied, "Yeah, but let's keep this between us."

Both Shawn and Abby agreed, and the men thanked the couple for their time. Soon Joe and Phil were traveling on the road back to Jonesborough. Both men sat silently in the seats of the truck, remembering all that was said at the couple's house. As they came to an elementary school along the route, Joe pulled off the road and removed his cellphone from his pocket.

On the third ring, Judge William Jones answered, "Hello."

Joe asked, "Judge Jones, this is Joseph Wales. Is Claire with you, and can you talk?"

Judge William replied, "Yes, Joe, we are alone at the house."

Then Joe heard William shout Claire's name. The judge asked, "What's wrong, Joe?"

Joe spoke into the tiny device, "We think Eva Mae and the boys have taken a small trip, and we need to know if Claire has any idea of where they have gone."

Just then, Claire walked into the room, and William put the phone on speaker mode. Joe heard William tell Claire that it was Joe on the phone. He heard William explain what Joe had conferred, then Claire responded, "Oh no... I haven't heard from her since Wednesday. She didn't say anything about a trip, but I've tried to be as nonchalant as possible when talking to her. There's no way I want her to know that I have let the secret about the wine out. Should I try to call her, Joe?"

Joe replied, "No, I don't think so... We don't want her to become suspicious of you and William. I'll holler back if I find out any information."

William thanked Joe, and the men ended the call.

Next, Joe dialed Sonny Rutherford's number down in the Smoky Mountains. He explained that he and Phil were now on board with the idea that the attackers were indeed werewolves, and that Eva Mae and the boys left the house with their suitcases in tow. Joe informed Sonny that they had no idea where the three were going, but maybe he should keep an eye out in the park. Sonny promised Joe that they would be on the lookout, and both of the gentlemen ended the call.

CHAPTER 16

Monday afternoon had come all too quickly for Ronnie and Ricky; the boys were starting to feel the effects of the changes their bodies would soon go through. It was late in the afternoon, and Eva Mae was simply driving the truck around the area, waiting on darkness to befall the mountains surrounding Maggie Valley. The boys were in the back of the truck hidden by the camper top as the vehicle traveled along the country roads. As the light of the day faded and the moon began to show itself in the peaceful community, Eva Mae could clearly hear the activity taking place in the back of the truck. Soon the thrashing and the snarling subsided, and Eva Mae knew the transformation was complete.

After driving for another 15 minutes, Eva Mae found the spot she was looking for. She eased the truck off of the road and placed it into park. Quickly, Eva Mae exited the vehicle and opened the camper top. Next she lowered the tailgate, and the boys bolted out the back of the truck. They scurried up the bank bordering the road and disappeared into the trees of the forest. Just as Eva Mae was closing the camper top of the truck, she was illuminated by the headlights of an oncoming vehicle. As she nonchalantly walked toward the front door of the truck, the vehicle pulled alongside and came to a stop. She heard a voice asking if everything was alright. Eva Mae realized that the man in the SUV was a local policeman. She smiled and explained that she had merely left the camper top in the raised position.

The young police officer smiled and told Eva Mae to have a good night. She grinned and returned the gesture.

Eva Mae climbed into the truck and started the engine; she sat there until the officer's taillights disappeared around the next curve. She eased back onto the pavement of the curvy road and drove the truck down the road until she located a good spot to turn around. Soon, Eva Mae was headed back to the little, quaint motel for the night. Daybreak would arrive, and she had to be ready to pick up the boys at the same spot just before dawn. After about 20 minutes, Eva Mae guided the truck over the little one-lane bridge and pulled into a parking spot at the motel. She slowly walked across the parking lot and made her way to the steps that led to the second floor of the motel. She distinctively heard the lonely howl emerging from the mountain. She smiled as she thought to herself, *The hunt is on.*

* * *

The six hikers at the old, abandoned "Ghost Town in the Sky" amusement park had finished the evening's meal a little more than an hour ago. For the last two days, the group had been exploring the mountains around the park and only had to venture out the next morning before beginning the trek off the mountain back to their waiting vehicles. Darkness had overtaken the area as the group encircled the fire, sipping on some hot tea and reminiscing about the adventure so far. All six people heard the lonely howl as it emerged from a distant spot down the mountain and raced by the campsite.

Rita, whose back was facing the spot the howl originated from, spun her body on the log and asked, "Did you guys hear that?"

The other five sat silently, waiting on any other responses in the darkness of the night. Then Alex said, "I've never heard anything like that before... What was that?"

Brian was still staring in the direction of the howl. "I don't believe that was a coyote or fox... Maybe it was one of the wolves they have tried to reintroduce to the area."

Then Donna stated, "Sounded pretty far down the mountain. You guys don't think it will venture all the way up here, do you?"

Frank noticed the concern in the girl's voices and replied, "No, I don't think so... They tend to shy away from any contact with humans. Plus, we all have our pepper spray to ward off any animals."

Cliff looked over to Frank and slightly raised his eyebrows; he couldn't figure out if Frank truly believed what he had just told the girls. As he turned back to face the fire, Cliff stated, "Yeah... Frank's right. It's not going to bother us, especially with the fire roaring in the middle of the campsite."

Rita turned to once again face the fire as it popped and sent small, red, glowing embers rising into the night air. It took a few minutes, but finally the group began to reflect on their adventure and all they had seen on their excursions on their daily hikes. Soon the group was joking and laughing about the silly things they had endured as they navigated the trails. Another couple of hours passed as the group sat around the fire, until Rita reached her arms high into the air and yawned.

The group decided to take a final bathroom break before retiring to the tents for the night; everyone needed relief from the amount of tea they had consumed over the last hours. As a group, they ventured behind one of the old wooden structures that made up the old, abandoned Wild West town. The girls made their way to the access way at the back of the building while the boys went to the far side of the adjacent building to find their relief spot. Soon everyone had finished, and the girls rejoined the guys to start back to the campsite. They walked single file along the side of the building until they met the wooden planks that the old sidewalk was constructed of.

Brian was leading the group as the campfire illuminated the campsite down the street. Just as he caught sight of the fire's glow, Brian saw a figure bolting behind the tents on the far side. Immediately he stopped and held out his hand. Rita was staring at the dirt, watching her steps as she navigated the darkened area beside the old building. Before she realized that Brian had halted, her face impacted Brian right in the middle of his shoulders. The rest of the group stopped in the shadows that the structure created from the glow of the full moon, high in the sky. Brian motioned for the others to take a few steps back so he and Rita could retreat back around the corner of the building, but he never took his eyes off the campsite.

As the entire group snuggled against the wooden boards of the building's wall, Cliff whispered, "What's the matter, Brian?"

Brian continued to stare down the street with only his head protruding from the corner of the building. He then whispered his response, "Something just ran by the tents on the far side of the tents."

Alex asked, "What, a bear?"

Next to speak was Donna. "Did anyone think to bring their bear spray?" she asked.

Most of the group placed their hands on the many pockets of their hiking shorts to confirm the fear of not having any pepper spray, then Brian whispered, "What I seen wasn't a bear, people... It appeared to be running on two legs."

Cliff chimed in next and asked, "You mean, like a person?"

Brian answered, "This wasn't a person... It looked like some kind of creature."

Then Donna reached around Rita and wrapped her fingers around Brian's elbow tightly. She said, "If you are trying to give me the ole 'scare Donna' tactic, I'll..."

Brian turned to face the group as he interrupted Donna, "I don't know what that was, but I'm telling you... something about it just wasn't right."

Alex asked, "What do you mean, not right?"

Brian turned to look at the campsite again, and Donna could feel small trembles running through her fingers as Brian's body reacted to what he had witnessed. After a couple of seconds, Brian turned to look at the others and said, "It was on two legs as it crossed the other side of the campsite. It looked like it was covered in hair. And I know this sounds crazy, but its head almost looked like a dog's head."

Frank asked, "What? Are you sure?"

Brian responded, "Yes, absolutely sure. I've never seen anything like that before."

Cliff interjected, "We got to get back to the tents and get the pepper spray, people."

Brian peeped around the corner of the building again. After a brief moment, he addressed the others, "Whatever it was... it was moving to the opposite side of the street. Let's go to the back of the buildings on this side and ease down to the campsite. We can get pretty close before we have to step out into the open."

The entire group reversed their direction but remained in single file as they walked closely to the wooden structure. Each member took small, calculated steps in order to remain as quiet as possible. Now Brian was at the back of the group and was continuously watching behind them for any movement in the shadows of the old Wild West town.

Cliff was now leading the group, slowly inching his way to the back corner of the building, ever watchful of the area that lay in front of them. As he approached the rear of the building, Cliff cautiously peeked around the corner in the direction of the main street. Next he rotated his head to observe what lay behind the buildings in the opposite direction and checked for any indications of movement. After several seconds of not seeing anything out of the ordinary, he slowly stepped around the corner. In his mind, Cliff knew that something could be lurking in the shadows, possibly watching the group and their movements in their retreat to the camp.

Rita could feel her heart pounding in her chest; she could now feel the trembling that her own body was exhibiting from the fear of the moment. She turned to face Brian just as he was turning from checking the group's back. Rita stretched forth her hand to Brian. He immediately nodded and gripped Rita's hand, and she squeezed his hand tightly and once again began to follow the others.

It seemed to take forever, but finally the six hikers reached the corner of the next building. Cliff stopped to survey the area between it and the next structure. The area between the buildings was dark, but the street beyond them was well illuminated by the rays of the full moon shining down from above. Brian, who was still holding onto Rita's hand, was intently keeping an eye out behind the group. So far, neither man had witnessed any movement.

After Cliff was satisfied with his observations, he began to move again, crossing the open space to the back wall of the next old building. Methodically, the group followed in his footsteps until all six were standing in the shadows of that building. Everybody leaned their right shoulders against the wooden boards of the wall and took a deep breath—all except Brian, who took another look behind the group. Cliff turned to face the others and whispered, "Only three more buildings... Everybody okay?"

Nobody responded verbally; they only nodded in confirmation. Each individual was clearly feeling the effects that the fear of the situation was exerting on their minds and bodies. Their only goal was to get back to the campsite where the fire and the pepper spray could provide some level of protection. Just like before the six hikers traversed the area behind that building, once again the group halted for Cliff to observe the area between the structures and the street that lay beyond them.

After a minute, the group began to move again. The process was repeated until they reached the back corner of the last building, Cliff peeked around the edge of the building and slowly scanned the entire area. There was no movement of any kind to be observed. The tents were all positioned in a neat circle around the fire, which was still providing ample light in the campsite. The wood was popping and crackling, sending little pieces of orange, glowing particles into the air, all looking peaceful and serene as Cliff stared at the campsite.

Cliff leaned his head back around from the corner of the building and spoke softly to the group, "I don't see anything around the campsite. We need to make our way to the fire. I don't believe anything will bother us as long as we keep it roaring."

Alex was the next to speak, "Let's go… I don't like hiding in the shadows of these buildings."

Cliff glanced around the corner, and after seeing no movement, began to lead the others from the building to the campsite. The other five followed directly in his footsteps, and the six individuals even picked up the pace the closer they got to the camp. In just a couple of moments, they were all standing between the tents and the fire. Frank instructed everyone to retrieve their pepper spray from their packs, but only two individuals at a time; the others could maintain a "lookout" while each duo grabbed their little spray canisters.

Once everyone was successful in the retrieval of their pepper spray, Alex placed a couple more sticks onto the fire. The flames slowly began to climb into the night sky. Everybody agreed it was going to be a long night standing by the fire, but nobody wanted to climb into the confines of the tents where they couldn't observe the surrounding area.

CHAPTER 17

Nearly an hour had passed, and the group had seen no activity around the old Western-style town. There were no sounds emerging from the darkness that surrounded them as the minutes ticked away, but each of the six people could overwhelmingly sense that something was not right. Every now and then, a gentle breeze would blow across the mountaintop and rustle the leaves of the trees, the same leaves that would change into their fall colors and give the mountains their picturesque view that so many would come to visit and see.

Brian, who was standing closest to the old buildings, turned to the group and said, "I know you people think I'm crazy, but how I described the thing I saw was true. It was moving on two legs and looked like some kind of a wolf. I seen it, guys."

Frank responded, "I don't think that anyone is doubting you, Brian." Then he turned to Alex and asked, "Do you think it could have been the thing we heard howl earlier?"

Alex shook his head and replied, "I suppose enough time has passed since the howl for whatever it was to have made it here to the campsite."

Donna was standing between Alex and Frank. She looked at Brian and asked, "The thing you saw... I mean, what kind of a creature are we talking about exactly?"

Brian shrugged his shoulders as he answered, "I really don't have an explanation, but I am sure of what I saw. It was walking behind the tents at a pretty good pace, on two legs like a person, but it had the appearance of a wolf. Like one of the things you watch in the scary movies about werewolves."

Rita let out a small gasp and said, "A werewolf? There's no such thing Brian."

Brian simply looked at the fire and back to Rita. "Listen, I'm not trying to scare any of you. But I know what I saw. I just can't make any sense of it."

Alex interrupted, "You girls sit by the fire and rest. We haven't heard or seen anything for quite a while. Maybe whatever Brian saw has left the area, but the rest of us will keep an eye out."

Rita glanced around the group and responded, "I can sit, but I don't believe there will be much resting on my part. My nerves are shot and I'm trembling all over."

The girls sat in the dirt between the tents and the fire, positioning their backs against the logs they had been sitting on earlier. Each of the girls stared into the orange glow of the flames but periodically glanced into the darkness that surrounded them. The boys kept the vigil of scanning the entire area for any signs of movement, secretly hoping that they viewed nothing out of the ordinary.

Another 30 minutes ticked away, and the group was beginning to feel that they had quite possibly dodged a bullet. Brian was staring past the back edge of the building on the left side of the street. Alex turned to speak to Brian and caught sight of the dark figure standing in the street about midway through the old town. He extended his hand to grip Brian's forearm and stated, "There it is."

Brian swiveled his head to focus on the creature. Alex, who was frozen in his stance, continued to stare at the figure lurking in the street illuminated by only the moonlight. The creature was standing erect on two feet with its arms slightly extended by its sides. It was standing perfectly still, watching the campsite and the six hikers. Slowly, the creature began to snarl and use its neck muscles to pivot its head in somewhat of a circular motion. But the red, beady eyes stayed focused on the six people at the camp.

Rita and Donna were still sitting in the dirt but were now intently focused on the guys' expressions. Cliff stretched forth his hand and said, "Come on, girls… Get to your feet."

Rita took Cliff's hand, and he helped her up. Donna grabbed Frank's forearm and used it as leverage to come to a standing position. Now all six of the individuals could clearly make out the dark figure standing down the street. For just a moment, time seemed to stand still. Then the creature rotated its head and arched its back to face the full moon, high in the sky. Next came the lonely howl that sent cold chills up the spines of the six hikers. There was no mistaking that this was the same creature they had heard earlier that evening.

The figure dropped its head and scurried between two of the old buildings of the town. It disappeared quickly into the shadows of the night. Rita's voice was trembling when she asked, "What was that thing?"

Cliff was the first to reply, "I don't know, Rita. Everybody remain close and be ready with the spray."

Then Brian said, "Maybe it took off when it seen how many of us there were."

Alex responded, "Maybe. I don't know… It ran between the buildings pretty fast."

The next sound that anyone heard was the impact of the second creature's foot as it collided with the dirt bordering the campsite. Alex wheeled around from the spot he was standing, in an effort to greet the attack head on, but he was a split second too late. As Alex was raising the canister to release the spray, the creature's arm was already well into motion. The protruding claws sliced into Alex's cheek and neck, sending droplets of blood splattering onto Frank and Donna. Donna screamed as the tiny, warm specks of liquid impacted her face. Frank reached over and grabbed Donna by the elbow. In the next instant, Frank pulled Donna away from Alex's side as his body began to fall toward the dirt. Immediately Frank knew that the main artery in Alex's neck had been severed due to the amount of blood that was exiting the wound, plus the fact that his body was totally limp as it sank to the ground.

Brian, Cliff, and Rita had seen the attack just as the creature sliced into Alex and immediately began to sprint to the shadows of the buildings on the left side of the street. Frank jerked Donna's arm so hard it nearly caused her to lose her balance and fall to the ground. In the blink of an eye, they were running in the footsteps of the others. For some unknown reason, Frank did not continue to follow the others as they rounded the back corner of the first building they came to. Frank turned left and began to lead Donna through a small, wooded area. With no flashlight, he was able to merely guide the duo between the larger trees that occupied the area to prevent any collision with them. The smaller limbs impacted their faces, arms, and legs as they fought to navigate the route that Frank had chosen. Donna was pretty much oblivious to the objects smacking her body after what she had just witnessed at the campsite. Both of the people's hearts were nearly pounding out of their chests, but Frank's only concern was to find them a safe place to hide and do it quickly.

At the third old building they came to, Brian noticed that the back accessway door was ajar. He bounded up the steps, tripping and falling just before passing through the opening. As he crawled through the door and came to his feet, Brian caught sight of the silhouette standing just inside the doorway. He raised his right hand to dispense the spray from the tiny bottle and screamed, "No!"

Just as Cliff and Rita began to follow Brian up the steps, they heard him scream. Cliff yanked Rita's hand and pulled her back to continue down behind the buildings. Two buildings down, they found the back door open to the old saloon where the Can-Can girls and the piano player entertained countless tourists that visited the park during its glory days. They eased across the wooden plank floor as quietly as possible, searching for a spot to take cover.

Brian had been somewhat successful with the first burst of spray, but it missed the creature's eyes and only sprayed the creature's neck. Still, the thing that stood in the darkness of the room could smell the unpleasant aroma that filled the air. Brian had retreated into the corner and was standing with his back against the wooden boards of the wall. His arm was outstretched with the canister aimed at the creature. Brian was gasping for air, partly because of the hasty retreat and partly because of the fear running rampant through his body.

The creature began moving around the room, jockeying for a position to make the attack. Brian's arm and hand followed every move. One of the boards behind Brian snapped as the second creature dug its claws into it and pulled outward, sending tiny pieces of wood flying through the air, Brian now realized there were two of these creatures. He exhaled a loud scream and slid along the wall toward the center of the room; this was enough of a distraction for the first creature to make its move. Before Brian could prepare for the attack, the creature buried its claws in his chest and ripped open the flesh, sending immense pulses of pain throughout his entire body. The next blow came as the creature lunged forward and buried its teeth into Brian's neck, and then it clamped down with the massive wolflike jaws. Brian's body went limp as his neck crushed under the force applied by the creature. The tiny canister of pepper spray fell from his fingers to the floor of the old building as all signs of life exited Brian's body.

As Frank and Donna cleared the small, wooded area and emerged into what appeared to be another walkway for the tourists from years gone by, they both heard the scream from the old town slightly above them. Both of the individuals had numerous scratches and abrasions on their exposed skin from running through the wooded area. The sweat was penetrating each and every spot on their bodies, producing a stinging sensation on their arms and legs. But neither of the people paid any attention to the discomfort that the sweat created as they stared up toward the old town. Frank gave another gentle tug on Donna's hand, and the pair began to travel down the path.

The walkway was barely lit enough for the two people to see as they moved along; the trees and the underbrush were preventing the largest part of the moon's glow from reaching the hardened dirt of the path. Frank was able to focus on just enough lighted areas to keep the couple moving at a steady pace, searching all the while for a place to take refuge.

Cliff and Rita stood motionless in the center of the old saloon. Cliff swiveled his head from side to side, trying to figure out what their next move would be. He could feel Rita's hand trembling in the silence of the old building. Both had clearly heard the screams coming from Brian a couple of buildings down. Each had listened to the gruesome sounds of the attack that had taken place. Rita's entire body was shaking from fear that had overtaken her. Her breathing was now coming in short bursts of inhaling and exhaling in the darkness that surrounded them. She was still alert enough to pause between the bursts for just a second or two and listen for any sounds of movement.

Without warning, Cliff pulled Rita's hand, and the couple began to move toward the open end of the old saloon bar, where customers would form a line to order soft drinks before the show. Once behind it, Cliff guided Rita to the end of the bar where employees had collected money for Cola or root beer that had been ordered so many years ago. Cliff whispered into Rita's ear, "We'll hide beneath the bar where they kept the glasses and supplies. Be as quite as possible."

Rita never uttered a word as she sank to her knees and slid into the space between the bar top and the floor. As soon as Cliff took one more quick glance around the saloon, he crouched down and crawled in beside Rita. He wrapped his arm around Rita, and she buried her face into the base of his neck and closed her eyes. For a moment, there were no sounds outside or inside of the old saloon; the silence was deafening as the two people huddled in the tiny space they occupied.

Just ahead, Frank spotted an opening at the end of the path where it met another section of the old park. The moon illuminated the open area that was before them. At the edge of the tree line, Frank stopped to survey all that was around them. Suddenly he realized that this was the part of the old park that contained the amusement rides that many of the younger visitors cherished so much. He could almost hear the screams and laughter of the thrill-seeking individuals as the rides performed their magical motions.

The metal skeletons of the old machinery seemed to be rising and trying to escape the clutches of the native vines that were consuming the area. Some of the seats that the riders were fastened into had become dislocated from the frame and had fallen to the ground, only to be engulfed in the foliage below. High up on one of the rides, Frank spotted one of the bucket-type seats still attached to the metal arm of the mechanism still sitting eerily in the glow of the moon.

With a gentle tug on Donna's arm, they were moving again. After wading through the waist-high foliage, Frank positioned Donna next to the metal frame of the amusement ride and told her to start climbing. Frank assisted Donna as much as humanly possible as he traversed the old metal frame behind her. Within a couple of minutes, the duo eased over into the bucket seat and nestled down the covered section where the riders of years gone by would place their feet. Frank leaned back, and Donna sat between Frank's legs and rested back against his chest. Frank wrapped his arms around Donna and whispered, "No matter what you hear... we need to stay calm and be very, very quiet."

Donna only nodded as a response. Frank was able to see the campsite from their hiding spot, but only with a limited view due to the fact that they were now positioned a little ways down the mountain. The fire was still burning and shooting little red embers into the night sky that were clearly visible above the height of the tents. The tents were still perfectly placed in their circular formation around the fire, but Frank could not see Alex as he lay there motionless.

Frank began to think about the moment the attack occurred as he watched the campsite—how quickly things had happened and how he was pretty sure that two of his friends were no longer alive. His mind raced as he thought, *What are these things, and where could they have possibly come from? How long had they been watching the six of us? Would anyone survive the night? Only time can answer these questions... but will time be on our side?*

CHAPTER 18

There had been nearly 10 minutes of utter silence until the first sound of something entering the saloon from the back door traveled through the darkness. Both Cliff and Rita could hear the clicking sound as the creature's claws impacted the wooden planks with each step it took. Periodically, the old wooden boards would creak under the weight as it moved around the wooden tables and chairs that still occupied the room. Suddenly silence filled the room as the creature stopped and scanned the darkened building.

Cliff tightened his grip on Rita as she pushed her face deeper into the space between his neck and shoulder. Then the second creature bounded through the door, except it wasn't nearly as stealthy as the first. It was snarling and growling as it made its way into the seating area where the tourists watched the shows up on the stage years ago. The first creature that entered the building turned to the second one and began to exhibit the same behavior. Next the second creature began to move toward the stage as the other one started to search the seating area for another victim to devour. Each one would occasionally lift its nose into the air, trying to catch just a hint of odor from the prey it was pursuing.

The creature closed in on the stage and bounded up onto the wooden floor that the shoes of the Can-Can girls would collide with as they danced and entertained the tourists. The thud of the impact from the creature and the sound of the claws digging into the old wood sent chills racing through the bodies of the two people hiding under the bar.

Rita eased her hand up to her mouth and slowly placed her index finger between the clutches of her teeth. She began to apply pressure to the finger, determined not to make any sound that would give away their hiding position. The sound of the tables and chairs sliding across the floor reminded them both that they were indeed being hunted. For just a moment, silence filled the room as the creatures stopped to test the air for any scent of the two people they were searching for. Both Cliff and Rita could hear the creatures sucking air into their nostrils as they desperately searched for them.

Next came the thud on the floor of the seating area as the creature leaped off the stage, and its feet collided with the floor. The two people could hear the clicking sound of the creatures' claws as they began to approach the bar. Cliff gently removed his arm from around Rita and whispered, "Don't move. Stay hidden here no matter what."

In the next instant, Cliff quietly slid out from under the bar. Rita tightened the grip on her index finger with her jaws. Cliff jumped to his feet and started sprinting toward the open end of the bar. One of the creatures jumped onto the bar and lunged forward to attack, but Cliff lowered his body as he rounded the end of the bar, causing the creature to pounce only into the darkness and collide with the adjacent counter attached to the wall. The sounds of tables and chairs scooting and overturning echoed through the room as the second creature tried to fight through the obstacles to achieve a position for its attack on Cliff.

As Cliff approached the front door, he lowered his shoulder and rammed it full force. The door was the first thing to collide with the wooden sidewalk, with Cliff's body not far behind. Cliff rolled across the sidewalk and off onto the dirt of the street. Immediately he jumped to his feet and began to sprint in the direction of the camp for no other reason than trying to escape the beasts. Unfortunately, Cliff was no match for the speed of the two werewolves, and the moment of his retreat was short lived. Cliff was frantically releasing the pepper spray into the air as he ran, but none of the irritating mist got remotely close to the eyes of the attackers.

Cliff realized the race was over when he felt the piercing pain of the claws penetrating the skin of his back. The sheer force of the attack sent him tumbling face first into the dirt of the old street. The next sensation Cliff felt was the second creature clamping its jaws into his shoulder and ripping away the flesh. He kicked his feet and swung his arms frantically as he tried his best to ward off the attack, but he was no match for the things he was fighting. As the first creature clamped onto Cliff's neck, he had one last thought that raced through his mind: *Maybe I've lured these things far enough away to save Rita.* Then the pressure on Cliff's neck finally achieved its goal, and he drifted into darkness as the creature ended his life. Next came the benefits of the kill as the creatures ripped open Cliff's chest and devoured the internal organs of his body.

Rita was now lying in an almost fetal position against the supporting wall of the bar; she was still biting down on her index finger when the first creature entered through the opening of the broken-down door. She clamped down even tighter when the second beast entered, and Rita listened to the hardened nails scraping on the wooden floor as they walked. She could visualize their every move as they took a few steps and then paused to test the air for any scent of a human being. The air being sucked through their nostrils and lungs was an eerie reminder that they were hunting her. The creatures moved throughout the old saloon, bumping into any table or chair they encountered as they crossed the seating area.

Soon, Rita realized that the beasts had worked their way through the entire saloon and were now standing next to the back accessway. Rita listened as the creatures tested the air one last time. After a second of utter silence, Rita heard the creatures as they traveled down the steps and into the darkness of the night air. It was at that moment Rita realized that she could feel the warm, wet substance running from the corner of her mouth, down to her chin. She had chewed through the skin of her own index finger in an effort to remain quiet. Silently, she searched the pockets of her hiking shorts until she found the small packet of tissues. She removed a couple of the tiny pieces of paper and wrapped them around the open wounds of her finger. Rita squeezed tightly around the injury and did her best to remain calm as she stared into the darkness beyond the hiding spot. She wasn't sure if the creatures would return or if she had indeed eluded them; either way, Rita knew it would be a long night waiting for the daylight to come.

Frank was the first to hear the snarling from the confines of the thrill ride seat. He saw the two silhouettes emerging from the shadows between the trees and the old buildings. Frank squeezed Donna a little tighter and whispered into her ear, "Don't make a sound."

Donna never moved, except for her eyelids, which she clinched together as tight as possible. Frank watched as the creatures began to walk in the direction of the abandoned amusement rides. Frank could only make out the outline of the animals as they moved toward them from the backlight of the fire, but right away he noticed they were definitely walking on two legs. When the creatures turned their heads to look left or right, the feature of the beasts he noticed most was the appearance of their heads. Even though it didn't make any sense in Frank's brain, their heads reminded him of the werewolf horror films he watched on the big screen while eating popcorn and sipping on a soft drink. Frank intensely watched as they continued down the incline to their position, stopping every few steps to raise their noses to test the air encircling them. Frank knew beyond a shadow of a doubt that the creatures were trying to locate him and Donna. Hopefully being this high off the ground would be an advantage to them.

Frank watched intently as the creatures approached the first amusement ride and began to search around the rusty old frame. Periodically they would stop and rotate their heads like they were searching for any movement in the overgrown vines, perhaps hoping that another victim would react from the fear of the moment and possibly try to make a hasty escape. It only took a few minutes for the creatures to finally make their way to the area below the ride that Frank and Donna were hiding in. Frank once again tightened his grip on Donna, who remained perfectly still. Both of the individuals could clearly hear the creatures as they fought to navigate the overgrown foliage below the ride. Occasionally, the duo could hear the scraping of claws as the beasts crossed the metal skeleton to search all around the ride.

Suddenly, Frank felt the vibration of one of the creatures gripping and shaking the metal arm of the ride as it traveled along the beam to him and Donna. Both of the people remained still as the search continued below them, even as the creatures snarled and growled in the thick undergrowth. Next, Frank realized that the creatures were beginning to move away from the ride they were hiding in, and he witnessed the two figures racing back toward the campsite, sometimes on two legs and sometimes on four as they rushed up the small incline.

Frank continued to watch the two beasts as they stopped behind the camp and one of them eased between two of the tents. All he could see was what he imagined to be something being dragged away from the fire and to the outskirts of the camp. Frank sighed as he realized that the object being dragged was Alex, and he watched the two creatures kneel down as they began to rip open the chest cavity of his friend. Frank tried to focus his eyes on the opposite side of the camp but would periodically glance back at the activity taking place; he wanted to make sure of the creatures' next move when they were finished.

Frank was amazed at how quickly the beasts completed the gruesome task of tearing open Alex's body and consuming whatever part they were feasting on. Even though he could not physically see Alex lying on the ground—a fact that he was more than thankful for—Frank had a very strong idea of what exactly was taking place. The creatures would raise their heads above their backs and peer around the area as they consumed the body parts. Frank wasn't sure if this was a normal activity or if possibly they were guarding the kill just for themselves. For a brief moment, Frank wondered if he and Donna were the only survivors of the group.

Suddenly, the thought was interrupted as the creatures rose to their feet one at a time. Frank focused on the two of them as they were silhouetted by the fire. Slowly, they rotated their bodies, searching in all directions. Then, one of the beasts caught sight of the moon as it sank lower in the night sky. The animal arched its back and spread its arms in the direction of the moon. Next came the long, lonely howl that echoed throughout the valleys below the mountain. In the blink of an eye, the creatures maneuvered around the camp and bolted down the old Western-style street.

Frank watched until the two figures disappeared into the darkness between the old buildings. He loosened his grip on Donna and whispered, "I think we are okay… Looks like they just left the area. We're gonna stay right here until daylight comes, and then maybe it'll be safe to go to the camp, grab a cellphone, and call for help."

Donna only slightly nodded as she replied, "Okay."

Rita's body tightened as the howl made its way down the street and rushed in through the broken door of the saloon. She tried to remain as still as possible, listening for any sounds that would alert her of impending danger. Little did she know that the creatures ran right past Cliff and the old saloon as they exited the abandoned amusement area. She had no way of knowing that the night's ordeal was over, and she was now safe. Rita would sit cuddled in the darkness of her hiding space for a couple more hours until daybreak overtook the darkness and provided a sense of security.

* * *

Back at the motel situated by the small stream, Eva Mae just started to open the door to the pickup truck when the howl descended into the valley. She smiled as she climbed into the seat of the truck and started the engine. In less than a minute, she turned right onto the main road that traveled through the town of Maggie Valley. Almost instantly, she applied the needed pressure with her right foot and sped down the road toward the spot to meet the boys. She wanted to arrive at the location to pick up Ronnie and Ricky before daylight in hopes that there wouldn't be any traffic in or around the area. Eva Mae didn't want to raise any suspicions by being either too early or too late; she only wanted the boys to get safely loaded into the back of the truck without incident.

Just as Eva Mae pulled the truck off of the pavement, placed the vehicle into park, and exited, the creatures emerged from the trees and the thick undergrowth. Eva Mae quickly opened the cover and the tailgate of the truck. The beasts leaped into the bed of the truck and scooted up against the back of the cab. Eva Mae closed the back of the truck and hurriedly climbed into the driver's seat of the vehicle; she started the engine and placed the gearshift into drive. In just a matter of seconds, Eva Mae was once again driving on the small, two-lane road, only this time she was headed back in the direction of the motel in town.

Eva Mae continued to drive until daylight began to overtake the quaint little valley, and she could hear the thrashing in the back of the truck as the bodies of her two sons began to transform. Soon, the noises behind her subsided and there was a calmness that came over the scene. Eva Mae spotted an abandoned, old gas station along the road that obviously hadn't been visited in a very long time. The price of fuel on the old wooden sign next to the road provided enough information to confirm that no gas had been sold at this location in many years. She steered the truck past the sign and to the far side of the parking area. Once Eva Mae turned off the truck, she grabbed the backpack lying on the passenger side of the truck. It contained all the necessities for the boys to get cleaned up and dressed for the trip back to the motel.

In 30 minutes, Eva Mae and her two sons were safely back in the motel room. The two boys, exhausted from the previous night, laid on the two beds and drifted off to sleep. Eva Mae sat in one of the two chairs that surrounded the small, round table beside the window. She pulled the curtain slightly and glanced outside. The small tourist town was starting to come to life; adults and children were scurrying through the parking area, preparing for the day's adventure.

As Eva Mae released her grip on the fabric, she turned to pick up her book. She flipped the pages until she found her bookmark. She placed her feet onto the bed closest to her and began to read. Eva Mae would let the boys obtain all the rest that their young bodies needed.

CHAPTER 19

For the next couple of hours, the surviving hikers endured the minutes as they seemed to tick away in slow motion. Frank only moved his eyes as he diligently watched the area leading up to and around the camp. He listened closely for any sounds that would raise an alarm that the creatures had returned. Frank observed the fire as it dwindled during the passing minutes. The camp disappeared into the darkness as the fire continued to shrink to a simple orange glow in the middle of the tents. After almost an hour of hiding in the amusement ride, Donna had somehow drifted off to sleep. Frank only imagined that she was totally exhausted from the night's activities.

The next thing that Frank realized was that the chirping of the crickets was being replaced by the sounds of the many birds that inhabited the area. He knew that shortly the dawn would overtake the darkness, and they could summon help. In his mind, Frank wondered if they were the only survivors or if, miraculously, others had made it through the night. Slowly the shadows of the old Western town began to disappear, and the buildings became visible with the naked eye. Frank sat silently for several more minutes until he could confirm that there was indeed no movement in the area.

Frank removed his arms from around Donna and gently positioned his hands onto her shoulders. As he shook her, he whispered, "Wake up, Donna… I think it's okay."

Donna's entire body jerked as her feet hit the side of the bucket-style apparatus they hid in. There was a loud gasp as she sucked in the morning air. But the release of the breath was much more controlled as she asked, "Are they gone?"

Even though Frank wasn't completely sure, he answered in a positive manner, "I believe we are safe now. We need to get to the campsite and call for help." Then he added, "Let's get to the ground. Let me get out of this thing first so I can help you on the way down."

Donna placed her hands on the floor of the bucket seats, and Frank pushed on her back. As she came to a standing position, Donna rotated her body and plopped down in the seat. Frank was next to come to his feet. Slowly he stepped onto the rusty metal beam that supported them. Once he had secured a steady foothold, he stretched forth his hand toward Donna and said, "Come on... Let's take this nice and easy."

Donna grabbed Frank's hand, and the duo began the descent back to the ground. Frank noticed how the vines were trampled all around the base of the amusement ride. The creatures had expended a great deal of effort in their search for the two individuals. Frank could not believe that he and Donna had actually gotten so lucky as to avoid their detection. The two beasts had been just a few feet from their position, right under the seat of the ride they were hiding in. As Frank stepped down into the matted-down vines, he took one more look at the bottom of the bucket-style apparatus.

Donna was nervously scouring the area as Frank stared upward. She turned to Frank and simply asked, "What?"

Frank replied, "They were right under us. We were only 20 to 25 feet above those things. We got really lucky, Donna." Then Frank turned toward the campsite and said, "I don't know exactly what we are gonna find up there, but we gotta call for help."

Donna took ahold of Frank's hand, and they began to wade through the vines and bushes that were trying to reclaim the area. Frank was methodically watching the placement of each step as they moved, ever hoping that some critter or snake wouldn't be present in the direction they were walking.

Rita hadn't closed her eyes for the entire time that she had been tucked in the corner beneath the bar. As a matter of fact, Rita couldn't even recall blinking during the two hours she had huddled in her hiding spot. She began to wonder about Cliff—was he dead or alive? Had he been able to lead the attackers away from her position and somehow find safe refuge for himself? What about the others? Was there anyone else alive on the top of this mountain, or was she the only surviving member of the group?

As the multitude of scenarios and thoughts raced through Rita's head, she barely noticed the pitch-blackness of the room beginning to disappear. The break of day was slowly starting to intrude on the inside of the old saloon, rushing in through the windows and the broken-down door facing the street of the town. The long mirror fastened to the wall behind the counter of the bar was starting to come into view. One of the wooden trim pieces that bordered the mirror had broken loose from the wall on one end. The piece was supported only on one end as it crossed the reflective glass and rested on the top of the counter with the other.

As the light of the room began to intensify, Rita could see a few of the old glass mugs that the soft drinks were served in still resting on the counter. The glasses were covered in dust, as was everything else that Rita was able to make out with the naked eye. Rita could see the large window on her side of the room reflecting in the mirror. Even though the surface of the mirror hadn't been cleaned in years, she could clearly tell that daybreak had arrived on the mountain.

Rita listened closely one more time while she tried to muster up the courage to ease out of her hiding spot. After just a couple of seconds, she began to scoot on her bottom from out beneath the bar, ever careful not to apply too much pressure to the injured finger or, even worse, to bump it against something. As she passed the overhanging edge of the bar, Rita gripped it tightly with her good hand. Then, with a good tug, she was able to position her feet beneath her and come to a standing position.

For the next minute, Rita slowly moved her head from side to side as she scanned the interior of the old saloon. The curtains on the left side of the stage were partially disconnected from their supports and hanging precariously over the front edge of the stage. The tables and chairs were scattered throughout the seating area in total disarray. Finally, Rita took a deep breath and began to make her way toward the broken-down door. Just before reaching the opening where the door once stood, Rita once again noticed the pain of her index finger. She placed her other hand onto the finger and gently squeezed it.

Just before stepping through the opening onto the wooden sidewalk, Rita stopped and leaned her head outside of the door to survey the area, looking first up the street. As she rotated her head to observe the area in the direction of the camp, the question of what had happened to Cliff was answered. His motionless body lay on its back in the dirt of the street. Rita released the grip on her finger and placed her hand over her mouth. With her hand still in that position, Rita took a deep breath and ventured through the opening.

Rita could clearly hear the wooden planks creaking as she moved to the steps leading down to the street. Down the steps and onto the street Rita moved, slowly placing one foot in front of the other until she was standing beside Cliff. His shirt was torn into shreds, and his chest was completely ripped open. Had Rita not dropped her head to look at the dirt, she would have taken notice of the missing internal organs and the violence that Cliff's body had endured during the assault. Maybe it was best that she didn't notice these things. The tears began to roll down Rita's cheeks as she whispered, "I'm so sorry, Cliff."

As Frank and Donna approached the campsite, Alex came into view lying at the backside of one of the tents. He was much in the same position as Cliff, lying on his back with his chest torn open. Alex's eyes were fixed wide open, like he was frozen in the initial moment of fear. Frank was now certain of what he had been watching from the confines of the hiding spot; the creatures were indeed feasting on Alex as the fire began to dwindle.

As they closed in on the body, they noticed all the red-stained dirt around Alex. Frank paused and said, "Oh, Alex."

Donna turned away and lowered her eyes. She was torn between holding back tears and the feeling of being sick in her stomach. Donna shifted her feet and looked up the street between the old buildings. Immediately, Rita's figure with her bowed head came into view. Donna grabbed Frank's elbow as she shouted, "Rita!"

Rita snapped to attention and peered in the direction of the camp. Next, she began to sprint toward the others. Donna maneuvered around the tents and embraced Rita as they met, both of the women beginning to sob uncontrollably. Frank approached the girls and allowed them the time to sufficiently release their emotions as he watched the surrounding area.

Then Frank asked, "Rita... what about the others?"

The girls separated, and Rita answered, "Cliff is lying in the street, and he's... dead."

Frank turned to look up the street. He could see Cliff's lifeless body lying in the dirt. Then he turned back to Rita and asked, "What about Brian?"

Rita then explained all about fleeing behind the buildings, how Brian entered the back accessway of one of the old buildings. She explained how they heard Brian scream and the ensuing noises of the attack as it was taking place. Rita told the two people about hiding in the old saloon and how Cliff lured the two creatures away from her. Then she glared directly into Frank's eyes, and another tear rolled down her cheek as she said, "I hid all alone under the bar all night. I was so scared, Frank."

Frank hugged Rita and responded, "It's gonna be okay, Rita."

Rita asked, "How?"

Frank answered, "We're gonna check on Brian. Then we are gonna call for help. We'll get off this mountain as soon as possible."

Donna moved her head to stare down at the ground as she said, "Life will never be the same."

In the next moment, Frank heard a familiar sound as his phone emitted the small ding. "How about I make that call first?"

Both of the girls replied simultaneously, "Please."

Frank walked over, unzipped his tent, and located his cellphone. The ding was a message from Emma. The message read, *Okay guys, vacation over, time to come back to the real world and go to work.*

Frank read the message and immediately pressed the call option. Two rings, and Emma answered, "You guys are up early this—"

Frank interrupted. "Emma, something bad has happened. Alex, Brian, and Cliff are dead. Call 911 and get us some help up here as fast as you can."

Emma paused for just a second and then asked, "What about Rita and Donna?"

Frank replied, "They're okay. The three of us are standing here at the campsite. Emma, please hurry and get us some help."

Emma ended the call and dialed 911. When the dispatcher answered, she explained what little she knew about the situation. The one thing she knew for sure was that Frank was very serious in the conversation they had on the phone. Next, Emma found her boss and explained about her friends on the mountain and informed him that she was leaving to assist in whatever way she could. Within minutes, Emma was speeding down the road toward the old amusement park on the mountain.

Just as Emma pulled up to the parking area for the old chairlift ride to the top of the mountain, she was met with a multitude of emergency vehicles. Each and every one still had their flashing lights on. Just as she exited the car, Emma heard the thumping sound of the helicopter as it approached the top of the mountain. She finally caught a glimpse of it as the helicopter maneuvered to land next to the old Western-style town. Frank had just stepped onto the dirt of the street after checking on Brian when he heard the sound of the approaching police helicopter. Frank thought to himself, *Way to go, Emma.*

The three people were airlifted down to the parking area, and after a brief examination Rita and Donna were placed into ambulances to be transported to the nearest hospital. Emma informed Frank that she would drive to the hospital to be with Rita and Donna. She hugged Frank, returned to her vehicle, and sped off.

Frank was then met with the daunting task of explaining to the authorities about the events of the previous night. After filling in the police officers about his and Donna's actions, he explained all the facts that Rita had conferred to them. Then Frank took a deep breath and said, "I know this story sounds crazy, and from the look on some of your faces—well, I'm not sure if a single one of you believe me."

One of the older officers asked, "Frank, are you absolutely sure that what you saw wasn't a bear or mountain lion?"

Frank shook his head. "I'm telling you, sometimes these things walked on two feet and sometimes on all fours. They had heads that resembled giant wolves and were covered in hair. These things killed my friends and ripped open their chests."

One of the younger officers asked, "Why did they rip open the chest cavities?"

Frank rubbed his eyes and answered, "It looks like some, or all, of their internal organs have been eaten."

The lead officer informed Frank that they would be in touch. Then Frank was placed into one of the waiting ambulances, which sped off as soon as the doors were closed. The rest of the day consisted of retrieving Alex, Cliff, and Brian from the top of the mountain. This was accomplished while the horde of authority officials and medical examiners scoured the scene at the old "Ghost Town in the Sky" amusement park. Countless photos were taken from multiple angles as the people searched the area, the strangest being the footprints left in the dirt where the soil was soft enough to allow an impression.

The youngest of the medical examiners secretly used her cellphone to snap a few pictures of the prints along with the partially consumed victims. She was very careful and made absolutely sure that nobody saw her taking the photos. Just before dusk, the investigators were shuttled back to the parking area via the helicopter. Tomorrow would be another long day of investigating.

At about 9:30 that evening, the young medical examiner dialed the number. The voice on the other end answered, "Hello."

"Is this Rhonda Billingsly?" the young examiner asked.

Rhonda answered, "Yes."

The young girl then said, "Rhonda, this is Sandy White. I did some of my internship training with you while I was in college."

Rhonda responded, "Oh yes, I remember you, Sandy. How can I help you?"

Sandy answered, "Something took place last night over at the old 'Ghost Town' amusement park."

"What are you talking about, Sandy?" asked Rhonda.

Sandy answered with another question. "Can we meet somewhere to talk?"

Rhonda replied, "Well, how about tonight? I'm just sitting here watching television."

The girls decided on a meeting place on the upper end of Gatlinburg and the time to be there. Each of them ended the call and began the journey to the spot they had decided on.

CHAPTER 20

At a quarter till 11, Rhonda pulled her jeep into the parking lot of the small shopping complex at the upper end of Gatlinburg, Tennessee. As she placed the vehicle into park and turned the engine off, Sandy opened the door to her little gray compact car. After exiting the car and closing the door, Sandy walked to the passenger side of Rhonda's jeep. She lifted the handle and swung open the door. Sandy looked at Rhonda and said, "Sorry to bother you tonight, but I would like to talk to you and show you some pictures, if you wouldn't mind."

Rhonda replied, "Well, hello to you too." Then Rhonda laughed and continued, "Climb in… I'm guessing that this is pretty important for us to be meeting tonight."

Sandy climbed into the jeep and adjusted herself in the seat. Then, after closing the door, she took a deep breath. After exhaling the air, Sandy began to explain all that she had rehearsed in her mind during the drive over the mountain. She started by saying, "There was some sort of attack on six hikers last night over on the mountain at the abandoned 'Ghost Town in the Sky' amusement park facility."

Rhonda interrupted, "I thought that place was off-limits to people?"

Sandy continued, "Well, I guess it is, but there are still some hiking trails that intersect the old park. Apparently people hike up to the old facility and camp periodically, mostly just locals that are familiar with the area."

Rhonda then asked, "But... I'm guessing that something happened out of the ordinary on this camping trip?"

Sandy inhaled and exhaled another deep breath and looked into Rhonda's eyes. "Yeah... Six local hikers were camping at the end of the Western town; you know, where they would have the Wild West gunfights. In the darkness, something attacked the group as they were gathered around the campfire. There were two of these things."

Rhonda was already visualizing in her mind just what the attackers looked like, but she wanted Sandy to give her the description without any assistance whatsoever. Rhonda continued to look Sandy directly in the eye as Sandy began to speak once again, "Three of the hikers were killed in the attack; somehow, the other three survived by hiding in the darkness in and around the old town. One hid in the old saloon building, and two took refuge in one of the broken-down amusement rides that was left behind after the park closed."

Then Sandy positioned her head to look out the windshield of the jeep. She closed her eyes. After a short pause, she began to speak again, "All three of the deceased individuals had their chests torn open, and it appeared that the internal organs had been consumed. You just wouldn't believe the story that the only male hiker to survive conveyed to the authorities in the parking lot at the bottom of the mountain."

"He got a good look at the attackers?" Rhonda asked.

Sandy answered, "Yes, apparently he watched these two things for quite some time. He said they were covered in hair, that sometimes they walked on two legs and part of the time on all fours, and their heads had the appearance of giant wolves."

Rhonda still offered no information while waiting on Sandy to regain her composure. Finally, Sandy sighed and said, "I heard a few of the emergency responders comment to each other that maybe the male survivor needed to be substance tested once they got him to the hospital. But... I'm telling you, Rhonda, the look of fear on this guy's face left no doubt in my mind that he truly believed every word he was speaking."

Then Rhonda asked, "Why call me? Why are you not at your facility examining the bodies?"

Sandy replied, "There were three medical examiners on the scene, and I only started working there about a month ago. So basically... I was told that we would examine the bodies tomorrow and I should go get some rest for tomorrow's activities."

"But you have some suspicions about the situation?" asked Rhonda.

Sandy smiled and answered, "I guess so. I think they just wanted the newbie out of their way while they done their thing tonight. Then, first thing tomorrow, I could handle the paperwork and possibly tie up any loose ends for them."

Rhonda raised her eyebrows, smiled, and asked again, "Why call me?"

Sandy replied, "I did quite a bit of my internship with you, and you are very good at what you do. I also trust and respect you—for your work and as a person. I just didn't know who to turn to, Rhonda." After a short pause, Sandy removed her phone from the pocket of her cargo pants and continued, "I took some pictures of the victims and of some strange footprints all around the camp. Nobody saw me taking these photos. I snapped some of them while holding the forensic camera in the other hand; while they are not perfect, they are pretty dang good."

Rhonda leaned over as Sandy began to present the pictures to her. Sandy used her index finger to swipe up on the screen of the phone to advance from one picture to another. She would pause to give Rhonda sufficient time to study the photograph and then repeat the process. No words were spoken between the women as they processed each and every one of the pictures—that is, until the final swipe exposed the picture of a little tan dog lying on a couch with its head resting on a small pillow that filled the screen.

Rhonda smiled and asked, "Did the hikers carry that couch all the way up the mountain for the dog to sleep on?"

For the first time since the girls had met that night, Sandy seemed to relax somewhat. She laughed and replied, "Not exactly... That's my bestest buddy taking it easy after doing pretty much nothing all day long."

Rhonda chuckled and looked Sandy in the eyes. Then the demeanor on her face changed dramatically. A look of seriousness filled Rhonda's eyes as she began to speak, "I would like for you to send those pictures to me, if you wouldn't care. I would like to keep our meeting and those photographs our little secret, except for a couple of my friends, Sandy. If I'm right, these things have attacked before. Once, right here in the Great Smoky Mountain National Park a couple of months ago."

Sandy responded, "That's okay by me... but I don't want to get into any trouble at work."

Rhonda nodded and said, "I'm not sure why the other medical examiners didn't involve you with the process that is probably taking place even as we speak. I'm sure that in an examination room somewhere there is activity taking place that would rival the busiest beehive the state has to offer. I also get the idea that you are not so comfortable with the facility and the people that you work with."

Sandy slightly clenched down on the right side of her bottom lip with her upper teeth. Then she removed the grip on the lip and slowly moved her head from side to side. She answered, "No, not exactly. I know I'm the new kid on the block, but I have the feeling that I am not quite wanted at the office."

Rhonda smiled and asked, "I've been informed that we may be hiring a new examiner for the office. Would you be interested in joining our team on this side of the mountain?"

Sandy almost got a little giddy on the inside as she answered, "Absolutely, Rhonda. Do you think you could pull that off?"

Rhonda replied, "As a matter of fact, I might just be able to swing the vote in your favor. Let me do some talking to the boss in the morning, and I will get back to you. But... don't mention this to anyone, okay?"

Sandy grinned from ear to ear. "You got it."

Then Rhonda leaned back into her seat as Sandy began to send the pictures to her phone. A million thoughts raced through Rhonda's mind during the process of transferring the photographs from one phone to another. When the process was complete, Rhonda explained all she knew about the attackers and the people involved up to this point. She politely asked Sandy to keep all the information confidential, and she promised that she would. Each of the women felt that the other could be trusted, and the meeting in the parking lot of the shopping complex came to an end.

Sandy opened the door and exited the jeep. Just before closing the door, Sandy looked at Rhonda and said, "Thanks, Rhonda."

Rhonda smiled and said, "Thanks for coming to me... I'll get busy on that offer first thing in the morning."

Sandy gave Rhonda a thumbs-up and closed the door. Within less than a minute, both women exited the parking lot to begin the journey home.

At the last gas station exiting the busy little tourist town of Gatlinburg, Rhonda pulled the jeep into the area on the far side of the gas pumps. She picked up her phone from the console and strolled through the contacts until she found the name she was looking for. Next, she placed her finger on the little icon to call the individual.

Sonny Rutherford had just turned the television off and removed himself from the recliner where he had been enjoying the ballgame when the cellphone began to ring. The annoying little tone roused Sarah, who had faded off to dreamland on the couple's couch. Sonny leaned down to pick up the little device from the end table sitting on the right side of the recliner. He looked at the name of the person calling and simply swiped up on the screen to answer. "Hello, Rhonda. Little late to be calling to set up a dinner date, don't you think?"

Sarah rose to a sitting position on the couch and started rubbing her eyes. "I'm gonna have to keep a closer eye on you and Rhonda, I do believe."

Rhonda's laughter could be heard through the small phone in the quietness of the room. "As a matter of fact, a dinner date would be fantastic. How about you, Sarah, Billy, and I go have a meal together tomorrow night?"

Sarah looked up at Sonny as he glanced at her for approval. Sonny always checked with Sarah in case she had planned something for the couple ahead of his knowledge. Then Sonny replied, "Sounds good. I'll get Billy on board tomorrow at work. Where would you ladies like to eat at?"

Both Sarah, still sitting on the couch, and Rhonda said "pizza" at the same time.

Sonny chuckled and said, "Pizza sounds great. How about The Maestro's Pizzeria heading out of Sevierville?"

"Oh yeah... Love that place. How about seven o'clock?"

Sonny answered, "Perfect. See you there."

The two people ended the call, and Sonny stood still staring at the phone. Then Sarah asked, "And just what is churning in that head of yours, Sonny?"

Sonny dropped his hand down to his side and looked at Sarah. "Little late for a phone call, don't you think? And just how many times have we been out to eat with Rhonda?"

Sarah was quick to answer, "Zero."

Sonny shook his head and said, "Exactly... Maybe she's got some information for the three of us."

Sarah responded, "Kinda sounded that way. Will know by this time tomorrow."

Then Sarah rose from the couch and stretched. "It's almost like you are waiting on a birthday present and tomorrow is the big day. Now we get to ponder tonight and most of the day tomorrow about just what the present is."

Sonny laughed and said, "Yeah, we'll know soon enough. I just hope it's a present that I've been wanting and not just another pair of socks."

The couple turned off the light and retired for the night. Sarah drifted back off to sleep in just a few minutes once they climbed between the sheets. Sonny lay on his back staring up at the ceiling of the room, which was slightly illuminated by the glow of the moon rushing in through their window. Suddenly, Sonny realized that the previous night had been the night of the full moon. Now there was a multitude of thoughts running through Sonny's mind, making the task of falling asleep nearly impossible.

* * *

Early the next morning, Rhonda opened the door leading into the lobby of the facility where she worked. She smiled and said good morning to the receptionist as she strolled across the shiny marble floor. Rhonda always wondered what went through the mind of the visitors as they entered the front of the building. Did they ever wonder what lay beyond the large wooden doors on each side of the receptionist's desk? Even though the décor that lay on the other side of the doors didn't even come close to that of the lobby, the facility was immaculately clean, and each object beyond the doors was in its rightful place.

Rhonda passed through the door to the left of the receptionist and was now traveling down the one-foot tiles that lined the hallway. Most of the employees hadn't arrived at the building for the activities of the day. A large number of the offices were still dark as she passed them on her journey down the corridor. At the end of the hall, Rhonda turned right and right away noticed that the light from the supervisor's office was illuminated. Good ole trusty Nelson always arrived early and generally stayed a little past quitting time.

Rhonda gently knocked on the office door and waited patiently for a response. To her surprise, the door opened, and Nelson invited her in. He closed the door behind her as she sat in the chair facing the desk. Rhonda was going to deliver her pitch on behalf of hiring Sandy for their team when Nelson began to speak. "I'm glad you stopped by, Rhonda. I've had something on my mind for quite some time to discuss with you. Actually, there are a couple of things I'd like to talk to you about."

Rhonda asked, "What's that, Mr. Delaney?"

Rhonda had never called the man by his first name. Nelson smiled and said, "We're in a closed office, Rhonda. Just call me Nelson."

Rhonda chuckled and replied, "Okay, I'll try. But I've never referred to you as Nelson to anyone here in the building."

Nelson grinned and shook his head. "Okay, out there you can refer to me as Mr. Delaney. In here, just call me Nelson."

Rhonda nodded yes and leaned back into the chair. "So, what's on your mind, Nelson?"

Nelson answered, "We've worked together for a very long time, Rhonda. I trust your work... and your examination techniques are unmatched. Someday, probably pretty soon, I'm going to sneak into retirement mode. The wife and I need some relaxation time together, especially after all the time that I have spent in this building. I'm gonna recommend you for this position when that time comes—that is, if you are interested in the position."

Rhonda was flattered and totally shocked at the words that Nelson had just laid on the table. She took a deep breath and replied, "I can't hardly imagine this facility without you, but I am honored, sir."

Nelson laughed. "None of that 'sir' stuff in this office either, Rhonda."

Rhonda grinned. "Sorry, Nelson."

Then Nelson asked, "Now, what was the reason you knocked on my door?"

Rhonda cleared her throat and replied, "I've heard the rumor that we may be hiring a new examiner for the office, and I have a name to drop into the hat. Her name is Sandy White; she did her internship with me here at the facility, and I believe she will be a real asset for—"

Nelson interrupted, "The rumor is true, and there haven't been any other names that have come forward so far. The job should be posted next week. Get her résumé to Human Resources. You and I will have the final say of exactly which candidate we want to hire. After all, I am the supervisor, and you are the senior examiner. I trust your decisions, or I wouldn't be recommending you for my position. However, I will give you the time to bring the new examiner up to speed before I bug out on you, Rhonda."

Rhonda smiled and said, "Thank you very much, sir. I mean, Nelson."

Nelson smiled and said, "Now, there's one more thing I would like to mention—totally off the record and never to leave this room. This has been on my mind ever since the incident took place. I didn't want to talk about this until you had ample time to decipher everything in your own mind."

Rhonda tilted her head slightly to the left and asked, "And what's that?"

Nelson leaned forward, folded his arms, and placed them on the edge of the desk. He began to speak in a lowered voice, "The two hikers killed on the Sugarland Mountain Trail… I'm pretty sure that in both of our minds we are certain that a black bear did not kill that man and woman. The wounds were not consistent with that of a bear, a mountain lion, or even one of the wolves they are trying to reintroduce to the park. I was also totally confused by the actions of the state; that may have been the quickest I had ever witnessed on the closing of a case. There are some things that just don't add up. And I apologize for being so stern with the instructions from the state on the case. Politics can change the events as they take place."

Rhonda was totally sure that the man was being up front and honest, but she still hesitated for a second before speaking, "Off the record?"

Nelson responded, "Absolutely."

Rhonda continued, "It's happened again."

Nelson's facial expression was one of disbelief. "When?"

Rhonda replied, "Night before last. At the abandoned 'Ghost Town in the Sky' amusement park."

Nelson asked, "Over in Maggie Valley?"

Rhonda answered, "Yes. Three hikers were killed and three survived."

Then Rhonda relayed the details to Nelson just as they had been presented to her by Sandy, but she never revealed the name of her source. She pulled up the pictures on her phone and walked to the side of Nelson's desk. She leaned over and placed the phone directly in front of Mr. Delaney. Rhonda then instructed Nelson to scan through the photographs. After looking at the last picture, Nelson leaned back and peered at her.

He said, "I don't want to know the name of your source or any of the people involved. Rhonda, be very careful of your movements; tell your source to do the same. Nobody is ever sure of the politics involved in a situation like this, so watch every step you take and be mindful not to step on the wrong toes. Cover your butt at all times. I believe there may be a side to this story that we know absolutely nothing about."

"I believe so, sir," replied Rhonda.

This time, Nelson didn't pay attention to Rhonda referring to him as sir. The duo agreed on the privacy of the conversation, and Rhonda exited the office. She entered the door and turned on the light for her office. She closed the door and ran the entire meeting with Nelson through her mind.

Nelson sat silently in his leather chair with his arms resting on the padded supports provided for them. One by one, he visualized the pictures that Rhonda had presented to him on the phone. He could only imagine what kind of animal was capable of inflicting such injuries.

CHAPTER 21

At 10 minutes till 7:00, Rhonda turned left into the parking lot of The Maestro's Pizzeria restaurant. Right away, she noticed Billy standing beside Sonny and Sarah's vehicle at the driver's side door. *Always the last to arrive,* she thought as she maneuvered her jeep into the empty spot on Sarah's side of the vehicle. By the time that Rhonda gathered her purse and cellphone, the other three people were already gathered at the rear of her jeep. She exited the vehicle and closed the door. Then Rhonda made eye contact with the three individuals and smiled. As she began to move toward them, Rhonda said, "For once, I would like to not be the last person to arrive."

All three laughed, and Billy responded, "You're going to have to be pretty early if you hope to beat us to a pizza joint."

Rhonda shook her head and grinned. The four people walked across the parking lot, and Billy opened the door. He graciously held out his hand for the others to enter the establishment. Once inside, the host was quick to grab four menus and instruct the foursome to follow her. Luckily, she placed them in a corner booth where they could converse over the meal without interruption. After taking the order for the drinks, the host walked toward the kitchen area and left the group in their own little corner of the restaurant.

Rhonda looked at the others and said, "I'm sure everyone is wondering why I wanted to have this little get-together."

Sonny replied, "Well, yes, as a matter of fact, we were a little curious. We weren't sure if you had some information for us, or perhaps you just wanted to test our social skills."

Everyone chuckled as the waitress returned with the drinks and informed everyone that she would give them a couple of minutes to decide what tonight's meal would be. The group decided on a large supreme pizza with no olives after a short discussion. All four people opted for a salad to begin the meal, two choosing ranch dressing and the other two going for the thousand island. The waitress returned, took the order, and once again scurried to the other end of the room.

Rhonda placed her hands onto the red-and-white checkered tablecloth and leaned toward the table. She raised her eyebrows slightly and said, "There was another attack two nights ago."

Billy glanced across the table at Sonny and Sarah, then turned back to Rhonda. "Where?"

Rhonda answered, "The 'Ghost Town in the Sky' amusement park."

Sonny shrugged his shoulders and asked, "What in the world was anyone doing at that place, especially after dark?"

Before Rhonda could answer, the waitress returned with the four salads. She placed the bowls in front of the individuals and perfectly remembered which dressing went with each person. After the waitress left the table and was halfway across the room, Rhonda answered Sonny's question, "Apparently, some locals like to hike to the facility and camp periodically. After we eat, I'll fill you guys in on the details."

Just right on time, as the four people finished their salads, along came the pizza. The waitress placed the pizza dish onto the center of the table and collected the salad bowls. She informed the guests that a refill of the drinks would be out shortly. Each person grabbed a slice of pizza and placed it onto the plates provided. The feast was now in full swing as the four people attacked the pizza in front of them. After about 20 minutes and two refills of the soft drinks, the damage to the pizza was complete. Only crust crumbs and a couple of pieces of green pepper remained on the pizza pan.

Rhonda told the waitress that tonight's treat was on her, but after a short discussion, Billy convinced Rhonda to split the meal between the two of them. After the waitress returned with their credit cards and the two people filled in the little receipt slips, the group exited the building. Once they were all standing at the rear of the vehicles, Sonny and Sarah thanked the two of them for the meal.

Both Billy and Rhonda acknowledged the gesture from Sonny and Sarah. Then Rhonda said, "Now comes your part of the deal, Sonny."

Sonny grinned and asked, "And just what exactly is my part, Rhonda?"

Rhonda answered, "You are going to have to get into contact with the two TWRA agents in Sullivan County. Somehow, we have to put a stop to this."

Billy asked, "What happened over in Maggie Valley?"

Rhonda leaned against her jeep and began to explain each and every detail that Sandy had conveyed to her in the parking lot of the shopping complex. She even explained the meeting between her and Nelson Delaney, but Rhonda was quick to add that everything she had divulged was off the record and totally confidential. Next, she removed her phone from her purse and presented the photographs that Sandy had transferred to her phone. The three people studied every picture intently as Rhonda scrolled through them.

Sonny placed his hand onto the back of his neck and gently massaged the area just below the hairline. "So... you're telling us that we are going to attack this situation with no assistance from any local or state authorities?"

Rhonda replied, "I don't know what else to do. If we don't stop these things, the attacks will continue to take place."

Billy was the next to raise a question. "What exactly are we proposing that our action will be?"

Rhonda replied, "At the very least, I think the next full moon, we stake out the house where they live. That is, if they don't take another little trip."

Sonny sighed heavily and said, "Let me call Joe and Phil to explain about Maggie Valley. If they agree with the stakeout maneuver, maybe we can all observe Eva Mae's residence from Roger and Ellen's house. People, we are going to have to be really careful with our actions. Just like Mr. Delaney said... Cover your rear ends at all times."

The group decided to let Sonny make the call to Joseph Wales the next morning. Maybe they would be on board with the stakeout operation. Hopefully, Roger and Ellen would agree to be part of the team, and the operation could be carried out from the confines of their home. The group called it a night, and everybody departed the pizzeria.

Rhonda in her jeep and Billy in his truck had nobody to share their thoughts with as they drove home. On the other hand, Sonny and Sarah had plenty to discuss as Sonny navigated the roads on the way to their house. What exactly were they going to witness during the stakeout? If something went awry, was there going to be anybody that would provide support for them? A lot of questions with no real answers. The only definitive conclusion was that Rhonda was indeed correct. These two things had to be stopped, or the killings would continue and possibly even get worse.

Early the next morning, Sarah awakened and slowly stretched her arms and legs while still lying between the sheets. Next, she rolled over to greet Sonny, but his side of the bed was vacant. Sarah rolled back the covers, positioned her body on the side of the bed, and placed her feet onto the floor. Just as she pushed off of the mattress and came to a standing position, the bathroom door opened. The light from the bathroom flooded the room, and Sonny's silhouette could be seen walking into the bedroom. Sarah smiled and said, "Well, someone is up early and eager to go to work today."

Sonny laughed and replied, "Yeah... just can't wait to get the day going."

Sarah replied, "I didn't even hear the alarm go off."

Sonny chuckled again. "That's because I was already awake about 15 minutes before that thing could even think about making that little annoying sound. As a matter of fact, I've been awake off and on most of the night. I guess my mind was still trying to cipher through last night's meeting at the pizzeria and trying to figure what my conversation with Joseph would be like."

Sarah placed her arms into the robe and gently tied it around her waist. Then she said, "Maybe some eggs and toast will give you the incentive to meet the day—maybe help you to decide on the correct words to convey to Joseph."

Sonny replied, "I don't know about all that. But I do know one thing for sure—my pizza from last night is long gone. I've already started the coffee. Let's get the eggs and toast going."

Sonny followed Sarah through the bedroom door and into the kitchen. The smell of the coffee brewing filled the room. After just a few minutes, the couple were sitting at the table enjoying the morning's breakfast. Periodically, Sarah would glance at Sonny as he consumed the food. In her mind, she wondered just what exactly was running through his head.

After the forks were placed onto the empty plates and the two individuals were savoring the remaining coffee in their mugs, Sarah cleared her throat and asked, "What time are you going to call Joe?"

Sonny placed his cup onto the table and answered, "I'll probably wait until somewhere around 10 o'clock. I'm not sure if this is a workday for him or maybe one of his days off. If he's not working, I don't want to disturb him too early."

Then Sarah asked, "Once you talk to him, will you give me a call and fill me in?"

Sonny smiled and said, "Yes, I will. You're stuck in the middle of this just like the rest of us."

Sarah grinned. "That's right, ole boy."

Then Sonny got a serious look on his face and added, "If everything works out and we go up there for this so-called stakeout, you've got to promise me to stay right by my side at all times."

Sarah responded, "Absolutely, Sonny. I've already seen what these things can do."

Sonny helped Sarah place the dirty dishes as well as the coffee mugs into the dishwasher, just like every other morning. Just a few minutes later, Sonny was walking through the living room toward the front door. Sarah was right on his heels as he crossed the room. Once at the door, the ritual for Sonny leaving the house on his way to work played out just like every morning before. A hug, a gentle kiss, and the *you be careful* and the *I will* words spoken just before Sonny passed through the door. A couple of minutes later, Sonny was driving down the road on his way to the Great Smoky Mountain National Park.

Later that day, at about five minutes before 10 o'clock, Sonny pulled the truck into the parking lot of the Sugarlands Visitor Center. He had been patrolling the road between the center and the entrance to the ever-popular Cades Cove entrance. Route 73 is an enjoyable journey from the visitor center to the turn that leads to the Cades Cove area. Beautiful forests line the road, and several hiking trails are accessible along the way. A crystal-clear stream flows alongside the road for much of the journey. Sonny always appreciated the fact of working in such a beautiful environment, always thankful that he wasn't doing a nine-to-five in some concrete old building.

Sonny strolled out into the grassy area beside the parking lot for the center and removed his cellphone. Next, he called Joseph Wales.

Two rings, and a voice said, "Hello, Sonny. What's up?"

Sonny cleared his throat and answered, "Joe, we had another attack in the area."

There was a moment of silence. Then Joe asked, "Where?"

Sonny replied, "Over in Maggie Valley, North Carolina, at the abandoned 'Ghost Town in the Sky' amusement park. Three individuals were killed, but three survived. One young man and two girls got really lucky. The male got a pretty good look at the attackers; he also gave a good description to the authorities. I'm not really sure if anyone believed the story that this young man had to offer, but one of the medical examiners sure felt like the victim believed every word that he was explaining to the authorities."

Then Joe asked, "Rhonda?"

Sonny answered, "No, a young lady by the name of Sandy. But luckily, she did her internship with Rhonda, and she reached out to her later that night. This is all confidential, but she took a lot of pictures with her cellphone while nobody was watching. She also took a few pics of some strange footprints in the softer soil. This definitely looks like the work of the two boys and Eva Mae."

Joe responded, "I was afraid of this when Roger said it looked like the three of them were heading out on a little trip."

Then Sonny said, "I think we know what their destination was now, Joe."

Joe's sigh could be heard through the tiny little device. Then Sonny said, "We've got to stop this, Joe. I'm just not sure what the ripple effect will be on any of this. Rhonda wants to know if Roger and Ellen will let all of us use their house for a stakeout on the night of the next full moon. That is, unless they go on another little trip—and then I don't know what we'll do."

Joe replied, "I agree. Somehow, we have to stop this. Let me talk to Phil. Then we will get in touch with Roger and Ellen. As soon as I get some answers, I will get back in touch with you."

Joe ended the call with Sonny and thumbed through his contacts until he found the name Phillip Weaver. He pressed the little call icon and waited for the response from his friend.

Three rings later, Phil answered the phone. "Man, I can't even get away from you on my day off. What's up, buddy?"

Joe answered, "Unfortunately, we've had another attack, ole buddy. This time down in Maggie Valley, North Carolina."

Then Phil replied, "I guess we know where the three of them were headed for their little getaway. I'm assuming there were fatalities."

Joe answered, "Yes... Three individuals were killed. However, there were three survivors, and the male survivor got a pretty good look at these things. Sure sounds like Eva Mae and the two boys took a little trip to Maggie Valley."

Phil asked, "What now?"

Joe answered, "The four from the Smokies want all of us to stake out the house during the next full moon. I'll call Roger to see if they are on board with us using their home to spy on Eva Mae's house. Hopefully, they will be, and we can all watch for anything out of the ordinary as a group from the safety of their home."

Phil added, "I don't think there is anything ordinary about this entire situation, Joe."

Joe nodded his head and responded, "Yeah, I have to agree with you. Let me call Roger. I'll holler back at you when I get some information."

Phil responded, "I'll be waiting on your call, buddy."

After the men ended the call, Joe began to search for Roger and Ellen's phone number. Even though it was Roger's cellphone, Joe had the number saved under both of the individuals' names. Joe rang Roger's number. After he answered, Joe explained everything that he had been informed of so far. Then came the moment of truth. Joe asked Roger if it would be possible for the entire group to invade his home for the stakeout operation on the next full moon. Roger readily agreed and even seemed excited about the secretive mission taking place at his and Ellen's residence.

Joe called Phil to pass along the information. Next, he called Sonny to inform him that the stakeout was a go at Roger and Ellen's house. Sonny called Billy, Rhonda, and Sarah to relay the information. Soon they would all gather at Roger and Ellen's house nestled next to Holston Mountain in Sullivan County, Tennessee. That is, if Eva Mae and her two sons didn't have another vacation scheduled.

CHAPTER 22

Early in the morning on September the 17th, Billy and Rhonda pulled their vehicles into the driveway at Sonny's house. Almost immediately, Sonny and Sarah emerged through the front door. Sonny then turned to close the door. Billy and Rhonda remained at the front of their respective vehicles until Sonny and Sarah approached. Sonny was quick to suggest that the foursome take his and Sarah's car, and the four people loaded into the burgundy SUV. Right after Sonny started the vehicle, all four people fastened their seatbelts, and soon they were headed down the road.

Rhonda asked, "So, how do you people figure this night is going to go down?"

Sonny answered, "Not too sure, but Joe hasn't called and said anything about Eva Mae and the boys going on another little trip. I'm hoping we can get some good video of these things to possibly encourage more of the authorities what we know to be true."

Billy chimed in, "Say we get some definitive proof, what then? Do we just waltz into the sheriff's office and announce that we have a couple of werewolves in the southern Appalachian Mountains, then ask them if they are interested in giving us a hand?"

Sonny replied, "Let's see what kind of proof we can get, and then we'll decide on a plan to present it."

Rhonda then interjected, "Yeah, I think that will be wise. Surely the eight of us can come up with a plan to present this to whoever we need to."

Billy chuckled and shook his head. Rhonda asked, "What?"

Billy replied, "I never dreamt in a million years that I would be involved in chasing werewolves. This is like something you would read in a book, people. We're talking about living, breathing creatures that, up until a few months ago, we only seen on movie screens. But yet, they are real and moving through the darkened forests of the land we call home. This is really hard to believe."

Then Sonny asked, "Would you rather it be a Cherokee Devil Dog from my people's folklore?"

Then Sarah turned to look at Billy in the back seat. "Or maybe a Bigfoot."

Billy smiled and said, "There you people go again, poking fun at my Bigfoot suspicions. This is exactly why I never mentioned the encounter that I had two years ago."

Sonny turned on the right-hand signal and eased the burgundy SUV into the parking lot of the pancake house. He placed the vehicle into park and looked at Billy in the rearview mirror. Then Sonny asked, "What encounter?"

Billy smiled. "One creature at a time, Chief. After we get this little werewolf thing over with, I might just let you guys in on a little secret. Right now, we need to eat breakfast and get on up the road."

Soon, the four people were on the road again, and right about 12:30 in the afternoon, Sonny exited the interstate highway at the last Tennessee exit before crossing the state line into Virginia. Next, he turned right into the Pinnacle shopping complex that contained a store for each and every person that visited the area, local and out of town. Soon he found the area that Joe had instructed for the group to meet at. He spotted the white truck with the two TWRA agents sitting comfortably inside while waiting for them to arrive. Sonny positioned the SUV right beside the truck and placed it into park. Next, he exited the SUV and walked over to the driver's side of the truck. Sarah and Billy rolled down their windows to be a part of the conversation.

Joe extended his hand, and Sonny gripped it heartily. Then Sonny said, "Being a park ranger hasn't called for a lot of stakeout opportunities. Kinda excited to participate in this one."

Joe grinned. "We do a lot of watching at the local lakes, not necessarily for werewolves, though."

Then Joe looked at the others in the burgundy SUV. "We haven't mentioned this little stakeout to the judge and his wife. We kinda thought we would see what information the group could obtain before we conferred with them."

Billy responded, "Sounds like a wise idea. How are we going to pursue this little mission?"

Joe answered, "Roger felt that it would be best if we all came on out to the house early. That way, maybe it wouldn't raise any alarms for the neighbors across the street. Possibly appear like we are just having a little get-together."

Sonny replied, "Yeah... that sounds pretty clever. We gonna head on out there now?"

Joe answered once again, "Yes, just follow me. Roger and Ellen are preparing a meal for this evening. Oh, and they said there were plenty of snacks to get us through the afternoon."

Sonny said, "Great, we'll follow you guys."

After a short journey through the town of Bristol, the two vehicles began the drive through Sullivan County toward the base of Holston Mountain. The four people in the SUV attempted to take in all the scenery as they traveled down the road. Several turns later, they entered the driveway of Roger and Ellen's house. Sonny slowly eased the SUV next to the rear bumper of Joe's truck and placed it into park. All six people exited the vehicles and began to walk to the steps leading up to the deck. Just as Joe planted his right foot on the first step, the front door opened. The two German shepherds bounded across the deck and raced down the steps. Ben and Jerry were really eager to meet the newly arriving guests.

The dogs startled Rhonda and Sarah as they made their way to the six individuals at the base of the steps. Roger's voice emerged from somewhere above, assuring the ladies that the dogs were friendly and totally harmless. Joe turned to Rhonda and Sarah. "That's the story we got the first visit too, but I'm thinking it would be a different situation if someone was trying to harm these two people."

Then from the top of the stairs, Roger said, "Yeah... that might just be another scenario. Come on in, guys. Ellen got the snacks all laid out."

After the dogs had completed the sniffing of each of the newcomers, they returned to the deck with Roger. The six people navigated the stairs in single file. Nobody turned to glance across the street at Eva Mae's house; not a single person wanted to raise any suspicions of their visit. Once inside, Joe took a moment to perform the introduction of the four people from the Smoky Mountains, along with Roger and Ellen. Next, everybody grabbed a paper plate loaded with snacks and took a seat in the living room of the home. The dogs simply moved to a nice, cozy spot adjacent to the front door and lay quietly on the floor. Ellen asked everyone for their drink order, and Sarah assisted her in the kitchen. Once the glasses were filled, the two women distributed the drinks to each of the other six people.

The rest of the afternoon consisted of the sharing of information and everybody's take on what the night may hold for the group to witness. Seconds turned to minutes and minutes to hours; the afternoon disappeared quickly as the eight people conversed in the living room of the house. As Ellen noticed the light of the day beginning to diminish, she made the announcement that it was time to start dinner. Only after a small friendly discussion did Sarah and Rhonda convince Ellen that they would help out in the kitchen. The women disappeared from the room while the men were left to discuss more about tonight's plan.

Once the spaghetti and the hot French bread was placed onto the counter, the group heartily began to fill their plates. After the meal was finished and the dishes had all been placed into the dishwasher, the group focused on the task at hand. Roger dimmed the lights in the living room, while Ellen completely turned off all the lights in the rest of the house. There would be several vantage points to observe from. It was decided that the women would remain in the house and watch from the windows of the darkened bedroom facing across the street. The men would gather on the deck once total darkness had overtaken the area.

Soon the light faded, and darkness engulfed all outside of Roger and Ellen's house. The women positioned themselves in the back bedroom with the two windows facing the house across the street. Each of the women had a set of binoculars to observe Eva Mae's residence, along with a single night-vision monocular to share between them. The men eased out onto the deck and sat silently in chairs in the pitch darkness while keeping an eye on the house and the surrounding forest. All of the gentlemen had night-vision equipment in hand, and Billy even possessed a handheld thermal camera to aid in the recording of any event they may encounter. Both Ben and Jerry followed the women into the bedroom and found a comfortable rug to lie on.

For several hours, silence filled the house and the surrounding forest. Only whispers were heard as the group of eight communicated between each other. Roger turned to Joe, who was sitting in the chair next to him, and said, "Maybe nothing is going to happen."

Joe whispered back, "I don't know... The night is still young."

Only a small lamp was providing light in what appeared to be the living room of Eva Mae's house. So far, no movement had been detected in the front room of the house. Eva Mae's truck was definitely parked in the driveway, and no heat signature was evident on the vehicle anywhere. The mother and her two boys had to be there, even though there was no sign of the trio so far.

Sonny was the only one watching the window on the right side of the front door when the shadow moved across the wall in the living room. Sonny softly spoke, “Somebody is home. Did you guys see the shadow through the right window?”

The rest of the guys focused on the window just in time to see more shadowy movement. Phil replied, “Something is happening. There’s a lot of activity in that room.”

All three women noticed the shadowy figures as they danced around the room, silhouetted against the light-colored paint that covered the walls. All eight people continued to stare at the front windows of the house long after the shadows disappeared from their view. Had Billy been pointing the thermal camera at the forest bordering the back of the house, he would have seen the two heat signatures as they raced up the mountain.

Suddenly, Ben and Jerry came to attention with the hair standing straight up on their backs. The dogs began to show their teeth as they crossed the room and assumed a defensive position beside the women.

Ellen, standing at the window closest to the bathroom, turned to the other ladies and said, “Something just happened.”

The night went silent as the full moon rose in the starry sky and cleared the mountain. The men on the deck continued to feverishly watch the house and the darkness that surrounded it. Suddenly, from the top of Holston Mountain, the long, lonely howl emerged. It traveled down the ridges and through the hollows as it penetrated the darkness everywhere. Just about 30 seconds later came the second howl from a short distance down the mountain. Immediately, all the men raised their heads and stared in the direction of the vocalizations.

As if on cue, Ben and Jerry began to growl again as they continued to stand guard beside the women. Ellen leaned over slightly and touched Ben's head. "Easy, boy... It's okay."

As she reassumed her position, Ellen adjusted her stance to lean against the wall beside the window. Something odd caught her eye. Had those been there the entire time? Surely she hadn't missed them lying there, she thought to herself. Ellen raised the binoculars and took a long look at the objects lying on the floor. Then she asked Rhonda and Sarah to ease over to her position. Next, she said, "Look into the window on the left side of the porch, then focus on the floor beside the chair. Tell me what you see."

After both of the women looked through the window with their binoculars, Rhonda replied, "That's a pair of tennis shoes, but there's no way those things are standing in that position on their own. They have to be on someone's feet, and that someone is lying on the floor."

Sarah said, "We need to tell the guys."

The women walked into the front room, and Ellen gently tapped on the glass of the window. Sonny turned to see Ellen motioning with her finger for someone to come inside. Sonny whispered, "The women may have noticed something. Let's check it out."

Once inside, Ellen led Roger and Joe to the bedroom to take a look at the shoes. Rhonda and Sarah explained the situation to the rest of the guys. After all eight were assembled in the front room again, the guys decided they would go and investigate while the women would remain in the safety of the house. Rhonda was quick to object, citing the fact that she had medical training and could assist if there was a need for it. The guys reluctantly agreed, and they exited the house, along with Rhonda, who took the position between Sonny and Billy.

The time required to come up with the plan had unfortunately provided Ronnie and Ricky with the needed minutes to cover the ground behind the house and enter the back door undetected. The six people cautiously walked by the vehicles parked in Roger and Ellen's driveway. Then they crossed the road and began the trek to Eva Mae's front porch. Once there, the group paused and took a long, hard look around at their surroundings. Joe was the first to traverse the steps; the others followed one by one. Ellen and Sarah watched the group's every move from the confines of the darkened bedroom with the binoculars.

Joe slowly leaned around the wooden frame of the window and peered through the glass into the living room of the home. He knew right away that all the medical training in the world couldn't help Eva Mae. She was lying flat on her back in a pool of blood suspended on the hardwood flooring of the room. Eva Mae's throat was ripped apart, and the woman's chest was mangled beyond belief.

Joe whispered, "It's Eva Mae..." Then as he turned to face the others, he continued, "She's dead."

Everyone was standing motionless on the porch, trying to process the situation in their heads. Sarah and Ellen both witnessed the shadow against the wall as it crossed the room. Just as Ellen screamed, the front door exploded from the framework supporting it and slammed into Sonny. The impact knocked him off balance and sent Sonny tumbling down to the wooden planks of the porch.

The creature lunged in Sonny's direction and landed directly onto his body. The creature drew back its arm to deliver the mighty claws to the neck of the victim. Just as the arm began to split the night air in its forward motion toward Sonny, the gunshot shattered the darkness. Somehow, Billy had drawn his pistol just in the nick of time and pulled the trigger. The impact of the bullet sent the creature to the wooden planks of the porch, where it lay motionless.

In the next instant, the window at the right side of the porch shattered into a million pieces as the second werewolf burst through it. Billy aimed the gun but never pulled the trigger. The second creature only took two steps across the porch before leaping over the railing and disappearing into the forest.

Rhonda focused on the first creature as the men continued to guard their position—all except Sonny, who was now resting on his knees with the palm of his hands firmly planted in the middle of his thighs. Rhonda was the first to witness Ricky's body as it began to transform back into the young man that he really was. Rhonda shouted, "Somebody call 911!"

Sonny looked at Ricky just as Rhonda knelt beside him and was utterly amazed as the boy's body transformed before his eyes. Rhonda started applying pressure to the wound as Roger called for help. Phil ran into the house and grabbed the small blanket draped over the recliner. By the time he handed it to Rhonda, the young man drew his last breath. Ricky's last action was to smile at Rhonda just before closing his eyes and exhaling the air.

Billy lowered his head, turned, and then sat down at the top of the steps. Sonny simply placed his hand on Billy's shoulder and said, "Thanks, buddy."

Billy only slightly nodded. In no time at all, the multitude of sirens could be heard screaming as they raced to the scene. In just a minute, emergency vehicles began to pour into the area—a couple of ambulances and several Sullivan County deputy cruisers with all the lights flashing. Even one unmarked SUV that almost seemed to arrive before all the others; this vehicle contained two men in khaki pants and black shirts. These two gentlemen were apparently controlling the entire process of events taking place.

Just as Sarah and Ellen joined the others in the driveway beside Eva Mae's truck, one of the gentlemen from the SUV approached the group. The gentleman said, "I know it has been a long night, but we really appreciate all that you people have done. We'll take care of everything here. You guys get some rest. Your departments will be notified of your superior efforts in the solving of this issue. And it would be deeply appreciated if this night was never mentioned at any time."

The man turned and walked away before any of the group could respond. They all watched as Eva Mae and Ricky were loaded into the ambulances. Just as the eight people returned to the deck at Roger and Ellen's house, the emergency vehicles began to depart the area. About 15 minutes later, the group said their goodbyes, and the four people loaded into Sonny and Sarah's SUV. Joe and Phil climbed into the truck. Both of the vehicles backed out of the driveway and departed down the road.

Roger and Ellen closed the door to their house, and Ellen made sure she locked both locks. Ellen took a seat in the living room, and both dogs lay on the floor at her feet. Roger continued to watch the last of the activity across the street from the darkened bedroom.

All eight people were still in shock over the events that had unfolded. Each and every one of them were curious about the speech the man in the black shirt had given to them. Rhonda placed her hand on Billy's forearm and held it for the entire ride back to the Smoky Mountains as he stared out the window. Silently, in their own heads, everybody wondered about the ordeal that had just taken place.

Was it really over? After all, Ronnie was still out there somewhere.

ACKNOWLEDGMENTS

I would like to once again thank my wife for her continued encouragement in the writing of my books. I would also like to thank all my family and friends for the positive feedback. Thank you very much.

ABOUT THE AUTHOR

Daryll Simcox has resided in the Appalachian Mountain region of Southwest Virginia his entire life. Roaming the vast forests that encompass the area, along with fishing, especially in the secluded areas, has tremendously aided his imagination. The stories, created by the stroke of a pen, have traveled far beyond the expectations that Daryll ever imagined. Any and all comments are welcome.

Learn more at Daryll's website, www.daryllsimcoxbooks.com, by emailing booksbydaryll@gmail.com, or by visiting Daryll's Facebook page, "Paranormal, mystery author."

Don't Miss the Next Book!

Once again, mythical creatures are roaming the forests of the Great Smoky Mountains National Park. But this time, there is a division amongst the individuals who are responsible for tracking and destroying the creatures. Somehow, they must come together as one to alleviate and cover up the fact that such creatures really exist.

www.ingramcontent.com/pod-product-compliance
Lightning Source LLC
LaVergne TN
LVHW010658110826
845149LV00014B/3151

9781970471281